Rescuing Raisin

Be sure to look for these other exciting books in the Pet Finders Club series:

Pet Finders Club #1: Come Back, Buddy
Pet Finders Club #2: Max is Missing!
Pet Finders Club #3: Looking for Lola

And watch for the soon-to-be-released fifth book in the series:

Pet Finders Club #5: The Dog with No Name

Pet Finders Club

Rescuing Raisin

by Ben M. Baglio

Cover art by Andrew Beckett
Interior art by Meg Aubrey

SCHOLASTIC INC.

New York   Toronto   London   Auckland   Sydney
Mexico City   New Delhi   Hong Kong   Buenos Aires

ISBN 0-439-68886-8

Text copyright © 2004 by Working Partners Limited.
Illustrations copyright © 2004 by Scholastic Inc.

12 11 10 9 8 7 6 5 4 3 2 1   5 6 7 8 9 10/0

Printed in the U.S.A.
First Scholastic printing, April 2005

Special thanks to Lucy Courtenay

Rescuing Raisin

Chapter One

"That's gross, Nat!" Andi Talbot exclaimed. "Tell me you're not thinking of buying it!"

Natalie Lewis grinned out from underneath a bright green bicycle helmet with frog's eyes painted on it. "My mom says I have to buy one," she said, admiring herself in the store mirror and adjusting the strap. "I think it's kind of cool."

Andi stared. "You *are* serious!"

Natalie kept a straight face for about three seconds. "Get real, Andi!" she sputtered, taking off the helmet and putting it back on the shelf. "Green is *so* bad for my complexion. This is more like it." She selected a sleek lilac helmet with flashes of silver.

Andi made a face. What was it with Natalie and pastels? *Give me a sporty red or black one any day*, she thought. "So what's your new bike like?" she asked as they made their way to the checkout.

"It's yellow," Natalie said proudly, handing the helmet to the checkout girl. "Kind of the color of baby chicks."

"What about the gears?" Andi prompted.

"Oh, yeah," said Natalie, nodding. "It has those."

Andi rolled her eyes. "I know it *has* gears," she said patiently. "But how many?"

Natalie shrugged. "How would I know? Come on, Andi. We'd better get down to Paws for Thought. Tristan expected us a half hour ago, and I want to help feed the rabbits."

Andi untied Buddy, her Jack Russell terrier, from the post outside the store and gave him a pat. "Sorry for the wait, Bud," she said, scratching the little dog behind his tan-and-white ears. "The Fashion Queen had to try on every single helmet in the store. We'll go through the park on the way, I promise."

It was raining when they left the mall, the kind of soft, misty rain that gets inside your clothes without even trying. Andi soon wished she'd brought her raincoat. She'd been living on the West Coast for more than three months now, and she still wasn't used to the Seattle weather after the sunshine and heat of Florida.

They headed for Main Street and the pet store where

their friend Tristan Saunders helped out every Saturday. Andi glanced sideways at Natalie. She was wearing new designer jeans, red sneakers, and a shiny waterproof jacket. Her blond hair hung sleek and shiny in a pony-tail. Andi didn't need to check her own reflection in the passing store windows to know that she looked like she always did — hoodie, cargo pants, old sneakers, shoulder-length brown hair that kinked around her ears, and a little tan-and-white terrier trotting at her heels. She and Natalie were so different, she thought with a grin. It was hard to believe they were best friends.

They let Buddy have a quick run through the puddles in the park, then made their way to Paws for Thought. A freckled, red-haired boy glanced up from a stack of boxes as they pushed open the door.

"About time," Tristan declared. "I was going to file a missing persons report."

"Whatever," Natalie retorted, putting her new hel-met down beside the cash register. "This was really important."

"So she can ride her new bike to school on Monday and impress Dean," Andi teased.

Natalie blushed at the mention of Tristan's older brother. "Like I care what Dean thinks!" she protested unconvincingly.

Christine Wilson, the store owner, came out of the storeroom with a smile. "Hi, you two," she said. "Any lost pets today?"

Andi shook her head. She bent down to focus on Max, the pet store spaniel, who came panting out from his usual spot in the window to say hello. "That's what I was going to ask you," she said. "The Pet Finders Club has been a little quiet lately."

"If I hear of any, you'll be the first to know," Christine promised.

Andi and her friends had formed the Pet Finders Club after Buddy had gotten lost, pretty much as soon as she and her mom had arrived in Orchard Park. Now, five cases later, they were beginning to feel like real pet detectives!

Because of the rain, the store was quiet for a Saturday morning. Natalie went off to feed the rabbits while Andi and Tristan helped Christine bring in several soggy cardboard boxes from the parking lot.

"*KittyKins*," Natalie read out loud, coming into the storeroom and noticing the rain-blurred label on one of the boxes. "Cat food, right?"

Tristan gave a dramatic gasp. "That's so clever, Nat! However did you guess?"

Natalie tossed her hair. "I'm naturally brilliant," she said matter-of-factly.

"Not exactly rocket science," Andi observed. She took a look at the top of another box. "This one's tougher. *Old Faithful*. What do you think?"

Natalie frowned. "Something to do with dogs?"

Christine came into the storeroom carrying another box. "Yep, and it's great stuff," she said, nodding at the carton of Old Faithful. "Max loves it. It's special low-fat food for older dogs, with all sorts of extra oils and vitamins to help with their joints."

Buddy sniffed his way into the room, paying particular attention to the box of Old Faithful.

"I don't think young Buddy needs it quite yet," Christine said with a grin, grabbing a clipboard down from a shelf by the door. "Could you guys check the Old Faithful order against this list of customers? They've gotten my deliveries wrong before, and I want to be sure no one's going to be disappointed."

Andi held her hand out for the list. "I'll read the names, you check the cans," she suggested to the others. "Ready? Adams, five. Carrara, three. Chang, nine."

"Nine?" Natalie echoed, looking up from the box. "The Changs have one hungry old dog."

"Farrar, four. Fattorelli, three. Harris, five . . . " Andi continued reading as Tristan and Natalie counted out the cans of food. There were about twenty names on the list, and the order came to eighty-three cans in total.

"You could make a great display pyramid with those, like you see in the pet superstores," Andi remarked, admiring the neat stacks of Old Faithful lined up around them.

"Yeah, but imagine the noise when Max knocks it over," Tristan said with a smirk. "Come on, let's get these on the shelves for Christine. Then we can go for a brownie at the Banana Beach Café. I'm starving."

"You're always starving," Andi told him, gathering an armful of Old Faithful cans and following Tristan to the shelves. "Tell us something we don't know."

"Hi, Mom! We're home!" Andi called, letting Buddy off his leash and tugging off her damp fleece. "What's for lunch?"

Judy Talbot came into the hall. "So that brownie didn't fill you up then?" she asked.

Andi stared at her mom. "How do you know I ate a brownie?"

Her mom reached out and brushed a couple of chocolate-colored crumbs off the front of Andi's sweatshirt. "Call it intuition." She grinned. "There's a casse-role in the oven, and a card from your dad on the table."

Andi ran into the kitchen and scooped up the post-card, which showed a picture of green mountains sliced with sparkling waterfalls. Her dad was in Guatemala that week, working on an oil pipeline. He always sent Andi postcards when he went to a different country, and Andi stuck them all up on her bedroom wall. This card was number thirty-two.

"Where's Buddy?" asked her mom, looking around the kitchen. "He's always under your feet at lunchtime."

Andi glanced up from the postcard. There was no sign of the little terrier. "Bud?" she called. "Where are you?" Frowning, she went back into the hall. Buddy was lying on the doormat with his head between his paws, look-ing very sorry for himself.

"Are you okay, Buddy?" Andi murmured, bending down to the little dog.

Buddy gave a sigh but didn't move. Feeling increas-ingly worried, Andi checked him all over for some kind of injury. When she felt his wet paws, something clicked. "I forgot to dry you off!" she exclaimed. Her dad's postcard had distracted her from wiping Buddy's feet on the towel they kept by the door. "Mom, look at him. He knows he can't walk through the hall until his paws are dry."

Mrs. Talbot laughed as Andi vigorously dried Buddy's feet. "He doesn't like any change to his routine, does he?" she remarked. "You should see him in the afternoon, Andi, waiting by the door for you to get home from school. He's always there at four o'clock sharp."

Andi gave Buddy's paws and stomach a final, brisk rub. "He's the smartest dog in the world," she said fondly.

Buddy sneezed in reply, then followed Andi back to the kitchen, his claws clicking lightly on the tile floor.

After lunch, Andi helped her mom clear fallen leaves and branches from the backyard. The weather was getting wilder, and as soon as she had made a sufficient pile of leaves, a mischievous gust of wind came from nowhere and blew them back around the yard. By five o'clock, Andi was hungry again.

"I'm going to Tristan's for dinner tonight," she reminded her mom.

"Tell his parents I said hi," Mrs. Talbot said, putting on the kettle.

Andi shook her head. "They're out of town today. Dean's cooking."

Tristan's parents ran their own real-estate business on Main Street and were often busy on weekends, leaving Tristan's older brother in charge. Dean was cool, and Andi really liked him, though his cooking was sometimes a little experimental.

"You'd better get going if you're walking," said her mom, checking her watch. "Don't forget your raincoat. I'll come and get you later, okay?"

Andi put on her baseball cap and the cleanest sweatshirt she could find. She couldn't compete with Nat in terms of the latest fashion, but she figured it couldn't hurt to make a bit of an effort. Then she wrapped herself up in her long navy-blue jacket, put Buddy on his leash, and headed for Tristan's house.

As she reached the Saunders' front yard, she saw Natalie struggling around the corner on a bright yellow mountain bike, pushing down hard on the pedals. Her helmet was slipping over her eyes, and she looked as if she might crash into one of the trees lining the sidewalk at any moment. Andi suppressed the stab of envy she felt at the sight of the bike. Like all of Natalie's things, it was top-of-the-line, with gleaming chrome spokes and at least fifteen gears. If Nat weren't so nice, it would be very easy to feel jealous that her mom and stepdad could buy her such great stuff.

"That was really tough!" Natalie gasped, pulling her toes from the foot guards on the pedals with some difficulty. "It's much stiffer to ride that I thought it would be."

Andi peered at the gearshift. "You're in the highest gear!" she exclaimed.

"I am?" Natalie stared at the knobs.

"No wonder you were struggling!" Andi laughed. "That gear's for, like, sprinting down mountains."

Natalie flipped the gears down about halfway, tested the pedals, and beamed. "Thanks!" she said. "I thought I was just really out of shape." She took off her helmet and found a brush in her purse, which she ran vigorously through her messed-up hair. A piece of her bangs refused to lie flat and stuck straight up like a small radio antenna. "Do I look okay?" she asked anxiously.

"You look great," Andi assured her.

"*Bonsoir*," said Dean, opening the door and smiling at them with a wiggle of his eyebrows. He was wearing a black-and-white-checked apron and holding a wooden spoon. "Zee dinair will be ready in about ten meenoot."

"What's with Dean's comedy act?" Andi whispered to Natalie as they stepped inside. But Natalie wasn't listening.

"Andi, you didn't tell me my hair was sticking up," she

hissed furiously as they passed a mirror in the hallway. "I thought you said I looked okay."

"You do," Andi protested. "It's only a piece of hair."

A strong smell came from the kitchen as they hung up their coats. Tristan appeared in the doorway with a bag of chips and waved them at Andi and Natalie. "I suggest you dive into these," he advised, glancing back at the kitchen. "Dean's making some French recipe that they must be able to smell in Canada. Mom and Dad promised him a camping trip next year if he watched me a couple of times this week. He's taking the challenge a little too seriously."

Dean's pasta sauce was full of garlic, pepper, and something slimy that Andi didn't want to examine too closely. Even Buddy turned up his nose at a piece she intentionally dropped on the floor. Andi ate as much as she could, fighting the urge to sneeze when the pepper got up her nose. She tried not to laugh at the sight of Natalie, who was trying to eat and smile at Dean at the same time.

Nat must have numbed her taste buds to not notice how bad the pasta sauce tasted. She cleared her bowl first. "That was delicious, Dean," she said.

"Naturellement!" Dean grinned proudly as he pushed the pan of sauce toward Natalie. "Please, have some

more. There's plenty left." For the first time that evening, Natalie's smile slipped, but there was no way she was going to tell Dean she didn't want seconds. Across the table, Andi glanced at Tristan, who rolled his eyes.

"I think I'm going to throw up," Natalie groaned from the safety of Tristan's bedroom a half hour later.

Andi flopped down on a beanbag. "If you didn't like it, you shouldn't have eaten it." She grinned.

"You've only encouraged Dean now," Tristan complained. "I hate to think what he's going to cook next."

Andi was sitting on something with sharp corners. She felt around under the beanbag and drew out a small hardcover book with very lumpy pages. "What's this?" she asked.

Tristan made an embarrassed face. "Don't laugh," he said, "but it's my memory book. For Lucy. I figured if I made a book about her, I wouldn't miss her as much. What do you think?"

Lucy was Tristan's cat. She'd disappeared several months before Andi had moved to Orchard Park, and Tristan still missed her a lot.

Natalie looked over Andi's shoulder as she turned the

pages. Tristan had stuck all kinds of things in the book — an old collar, even a small, star-shaped cat biscuit. Lots of pictures of the pretty, tabby-striped cat littered the pages: Lucy chasing a ball, Lucy eating anchovies, Lucy climbing through an impossibly small window, with her nose peeping out at the camera.

"How did she do that?" Natalie asked, impressed by the last picture. "I couldn't get my little finger through that space."

"Cats don't have collarbones," Tristan said, eager to share his cat facts with the others. "Pretty useful if you're in a tight spot."

"It's lovely," said Andi, handing the book to Tristan.

"So you don't think it's sappy?" Tristan asked.

Andi shrugged. "Sure, it's sappy. But what's wrong with that?" She dropped a kiss on Buddy's head. "It's okay to be sappy about animals. They look this cute for a reason, you know."

"I know," Tristan sighed, looking at Buddy longingly.

"Hey, are you okay?" Natalie asked.

Tristan rubbed his face quickly. "Just a bit of dust in my eye," he said. "It's no big deal."

Andi wasn't convinced. She glanced at Natalie, who shrugged, as if she felt equally helpless. Lucy had been

missing for so long, they knew there was no point looking for her. The Pet Finders Club focused on pets who
had only just disappeared, when the trail was still
warm. But that didn't make it easier to accept that there
was nothing they could do for Tristan.

Chapter Two

The wind tried to snatch Andi's hat off her head as she jumped out of her mom's car at school on Monday. She pulled the hat firmly over her ears and sank her chin into her scarf as she ran onto the lawn in front of the school. Tristan was standing with Dean outside the main doors, stamping his feet and rubbing his hands.

"Look out," Tristan warned as Andi came over. He nodded toward the street. "Natalie's coming. Do you think we should take cover?"

Natalie sailed into the parking lot on her bike much too fast, her front wheels wobbling as she bumped over the curb. Andi held her breath as the wheels swerved left, then right. Somehow Natalie managed to slow the bike down and came to a breathless stop next to Tristan and Dean.

"You're getting better at that," Andi said admiringly.

"I know," Natalie boasted, glancing at Dean. "I've got the gears down now. I — oh — " Her triumphant smile faded as she tried to get her feet out of the foot guards on the pedals. The bike stood upright for about two seconds before it keeled over and shoved Natalie into the bushes beside the path.

"World class," Tristan laughed as he and Dean helped a red-faced Natalie out of the shrubs. Too humiliated to reply, she snatched off her helmet — which had fallen unflatteringly over her eyes — and marched up the sidewalk toward the doors.

Natalie was still blushing when Andi followed her inside. "That was so embarrassing," she muttered. "Don't tell anyone else that happened. Please? I'm sure no one noticed besides Tris and Dean."

When they walked into their homeroom, filled with kids rifling through backpacks or slurping bottles of juice, Andi was just about to say that it looked like Natalie was right. But then their classmate, Chen, yelled across the room to them, "Nice one, Natalie! What did you do, glue your feet to the pedals?"

Determined not to give in, Natalie rode her bike to school on Tuesday morning as well, ignoring the jeers as she swung into the yard. Andi was relieved to see that she'd mastered the foot guards and lifted her feet off the pedals before putting on the brakes.

That afternoon, Andi and Tristan waited patiently as Natalie unlocked her bike and buckled on her helmet. Tristan rolled his skateboard along a couple of yards and paused to look back at Andi. "Seems you're the only one without wheels now," he said with a grin.

Andi tightened the laces on her sneakers. "I don't need wheels to get to Paws for Thought," she said, straightening up. They were going to the pet store to get some food for Jet, Natalie's black Lab. "It's not far, and it's good training. I'll race you if you want."

But Tristan wasn't listening. A tabby-and-white cat was sitting in a yard opposite the school, carefully washing its face. He took a step forward. The cat looked up and gave a wide yawn, showing sharp teeth and a pale pink tongue.

"Oh." Tristan stopped abruptly. "I thought . . . "

Andi put her hand on his arm. "You thought it was Lucy, right?" she guessed.

Tristan angrily kicked the curb. "I'm so ridiculous," he said. "Every time I see a tabby cat, I think it's Lucy. Sometimes they don't even look like her." He pointed at the cat. "Like that one. The tabby stripes are all wrong. Lucy's are much closer together."

"I'm sorry, Tristan," Andi said sincerely. "It must really hurt. But remember, you have that great memory book at home now. That's something you can treasure forever."

Natalie swung her leg over her bike and Tristan gave a push on his skateboard so that he whizzed along the sidewalk beside her. Breaking into an easy jog, Andi ran beside them, shouting precautions to Natalie if it looked like she was getting careless with her steering.

Andi's long legs kept up with Tristan and Natalie easily for the first ten minutes. Then Natalie started getting more confident, speeding up to overtake Tristan. Andi pushed a little harder, determined to keep up.

Fifteen minutes later, they arrived at Paws for Thought. Tristan flipped his skateboard up and caught it with one hand, while Natalie carefully chained her bike to the railing beside the pet store. Andi rested her hands on her knees, catching her breath. Racing a bike and a skateboard had been much harder than she'd expected.

"Not tired, are you, Andi?" Tristan teased, pushing open the pet-store door. "Surely not you, the girl with legs of steel?"

"I could do it again right now," Andi retorted.

"Well, once we've picked up the food, maybe we can

race over to your place, Andi," said Natalie. "I'm really getting the hang of the bike now."

Christine was on the phone when they went inside. She waved them in with her free hand. "I'm just calling to let you know your delivery of Old Faithful has arrived, Mrs. Harris," she was saying. "Five cans, just as you ordered."

Then she paused and frowned. "Missing?" she said. "Since when?"

Andi raised her eyebrows at the others. This sounded like something that just might interest them.

Christine listened for a few more seconds. "I'm so sorry to hear that," she said. "But I might be able to help you, Mrs. Harris. Have you heard of the Pet Finders Club?"

Andi high-fived the others. A new case!

"Yes, they really helped me when half the animals disappeared from the store a couple of months back," Christine was saying. She covered the receiver for a moment. "Is there any chance you three could call on Mrs. Harris?" she asked. "Their dog, Raisin, vanished yesterday. She'd really like to meet with you."

"We can go over there now," Andi suggested, forgetting her aching legs at once. She glanced at the others, who nodded in agreement.

Christine scribbled down a set of directions, then hung up the phone. "Raisin's an elderly Dalmatian," she explained. "The Harrises are crazy about him. If you can do anything to help, they would be really grateful."

They quickly loaded the box of Jet's food into Natalie's backpack and waved good-bye to Christine. Rejuvenated with a fresh burst of energy, Andi ran ahead of Tristan and Natalie, though it wasn't long before they caught up. She watched them speed up the street, Nat bent over the handlebars like she was riding in the Tour de France, and Tris stabbing the ground with his right foot every few moments to pump up his speed. Although she loved running, Andi couldn't help feeling that, sometimes, wheels had their advantages.

The Harrises lived ten minutes from Paws for Thought, at the top of a steep hill that wound slowly around several sharp corners. With the extra weight of the dog food, Natalie had to dismount halfway up and push her bike. Andi was thankful for the chance to slow down and walk alongside her. Tristan stayed on his skateboard the whole way, pushing steadily upward, though he looked red-faced and out of breath at the top of the hill.

Mrs. Harris was waiting anxiously for them outside her house. She was an auburn-haired woman in her fifties, Andi guessed, with a soft, powdered face and worried brown eyes. "Thank you for coming so quickly," she said, ushering them inside. The hallway smelled of lavender and furniture polish. "My husband and I have been so worried about Raisin."

"We're glad to help," said Tristan. "I'm Tristan Saunders, by the way, and these are the other Pet Finders, Andi Talbot and Natalie Lewis."

Mr. Harris stood up from his armchair as they entered the living room. He had thinning gray hair and was wearing a green-checked shirt and a similarly worried expression.

Andi looked around. Every spare space in the room — on the wall and on surfaces — was filled with photographs. "Are all these pictures of Raisin?" she asked.

"Most of them, yes," said Mrs. Harris, picking up a photograph and wiping a speck of dust off the glass. "The ones beside the door are of Raisin's mother, Dapple, and his grandmother, Speckle. My husband and I have always had Dalmatians. They're such lovely dogs."

Andi admired the photographs, which showed Raisin leaping around the Harrises' yard, or digging in a flowerbed, or curled up in a basket in a tangle of long limbs and distinctive black-and-white fur.

"Is he called Raisin because of his spots?" she guessed.

Mrs. Harris nodded. "That and the fact that he loves raisins," she said. "They're his favorite snack." She caught Andi's surprised expression. "Oh, don't worry," she assured her. "Raisins are a little unusual, but they're good treats for dogs. Much healthier than doggy bones!"

"Christine said Raisin was an older dog," Tristan said, peering at a photograph of Raisin leaping in the air to catch a ball. "Was he much younger here?"

"That was taken earlier this year," Mr. Harris said. "You wouldn't believe his age if you met him. That food we get from Christine's store really seems to help. The only thing he won't do is climb the stairs. His joints aren't really up to that."

Andi picked up a photograph that was sitting on the mantelpiece. It showed Raisin smiling up at the camera, his tongue lolling out and a goofy expression on his face. "Do you think we could borrow this?" she asked. "We'll make a poster for Raisin, and it would be great to have a photograph of him."

"Of course," said Mr. Harris.

"The police couldn't really help," Mrs. Harris ex-

plained, bringing glasses of juice for the kids. "They told me that he would probably turn up, since he's not in the habit of wandering off. Maybe they're right, but he's been missing for twenty-four hours now. It's just not like him."

Natalie took a sip of her juice. "When did you last see him?"

"It was yesterday afternoon, around five o'clock," Mrs. Harris said. "I know that because I'd just been listening to the news on the radio. My husband was out and I was here on my own. Anyway, I threw a toy for Raisin in the backyard, and he ran off to pick it up, just like he always does. But then the telephone rang. When I came back outside, he was gone." She sighed heavily.

Mr. Harris came over and put his arm around his wife's shoulders as she fumbled in her pocket for a handkerchief. She blew her nose, and gave Andi a watery smile. "I'm so sorry," she said. "It's just — we love Raisin so much, you see."

Tristan pulled a shiny red notebook and a pen out of his backpack with a flourish. "Would you mind telling us what you were doing yesterday at five o'clock, Mr. Harris?" he asked, sounding very official.

"I had taken the day off work and was at the garden center buying some sand," said Mr. Harris. "They were having a one-day sale, and the savings were too good to miss. I'm building a play pit for Raisin in the yard. Dalmatians need plenty of exercise, and Raisin loves digging. We thought it would be fun to have a special place for him, full of interesting toys to dig up."

"My dog, Buddy, loves digging, too," said Andi. "He dug right under our fence once. Terriers will get around anything if there's something to chase on the other side!"

"Raisin never did that," Mr. Harris assured her. "He wasn't — isn't — that kind of dog. . . . " His voice trailed away, and his wife patted his hand comfortingly.

"Would you bring your dog over sometime, Andi?" asked Mrs. Harris, changing the subject. "Maybe he'll pick up Raisin's scent in the yard and help you find him."

"Uh . . . sure," Andi said uncertainly. She wasn't too hopeful that Buddy would be able to do that, but she didn't feel like she could turn Mrs. Harris down when she seemed ready to try anything to find her missing dog.

"We'll start by looking around here," said Tristan, closing the notebook and shoving it into his backpack. "Then we'll make posters to put up all around town. I

promise we'll let you know as soon as we hear from anyone who might have seen him."

"Thank you," said Mr. Harris. "We're very fortunate to
have you. Christine said you'd done great work finding
other missing pets! I'm sure you'll find Raisin in no
time."

Tristan swallowed hard, and Andi guessed he was
feeling the pressure of the Harrises' expectations.

"They were so nice," Natalie sighed as the Harrises
closed the front door behind them. "I just hope we can
help them find Raisin."

Andi pulled the photograph out of her pocket and
studied it. "Let's get started right away," she suggested.
"The Harrises said they've only asked their closest
neighbors about Raisin."

They moved slowly down the street, ringing doorbells
and showing people the photograph. Several of the Harrises' neighbors recognized the dog quickly, but they
didn't remember seeing him the day before. The Pet
Finders tried to come up with some different scenarios
as they made their way along the houses. Was Raisin
just lost, or had he been stolen?

When they reached the last house on the street, Andi

glanced at the others. "Cross your fingers," she said. "This is our last chance."

She rang the bell. A red-haired girl about their own age came to the door.

"We're looking for a missing dog," said Andi, holding out the photograph. "I don't suppose you saw him yesterday, did you?"

The girl glanced at the picture. "Sure, I did," she said casually. "He's pretty unmistakable with all those weird spots, don't you think?"

Chapter Three

Andi's heart jumped. This was their best lead yet! Too bad the girl didn't seem to realize that Dalmatians were beautiful *because* of their spots.

"What time was that?" Andi asked.

"Five o'clock," said the girl promptly. She indicated the clock standing in the hallway behind her. "That clock struck the hour right at the end of the show I was watching. I missed a really good part. Then I went to make some cocoa and looked out the window." She pointed to the end of the street, where the road curved away out of sight. "He was heading that way. I didn't think he was lost because he looked like he knew where he was going. You know, head up, ears pricked, like Lassie going to rescue some kid."

Andi nodded. It definitely sounded like Raisin, but

where could he have been going on his own so purposefully?

"We've almost solved the case already, and we just started!" Natalie said jubilantly as they hurried back down the street to tell the Harrises.

"Not so fast," Andi cautioned as they turned into the Harrises' front yard. "We don't know *where* Raisin was going. We just know which direction he was headed, okay?"

"He was on the road?" exclaimed Mrs. Harris, sounding horrified when they told her about the sighting. "But what about the traffic?"

"Our witness said he looked fine," Tristan said hastily. "We'll come back tomorrow after school and see if we can trace Raisin any further. It's getting a little dark now to keep looking."

Mr. Harris bit his lip. "Dalmatians can keep running for hours," he said unhappily. "Did you know they were bred to run alongside carriages in the old days? I hope he doesn't go too far. It could be dangerous out there."

"If you'll be around tomorrow, will you stop by?" Mr. Harris asked hopefully, showing them to the door. "And bring your dogs — Buddy and Jet, wasn't it? We miss having a dog in the house."

"They're so worried," Natalie said tearfully as they headed back down the hill toward Andi's house. "I feel awful for them."

"At least we've had a sighting," Andi said, trying to sound encouraging. "That's good, isn't it?"

"I'm looking forward to seeing their backyard," said Tristan, bouncing his skateboard up on the curb and down again. "It sounds great, with the play pit and all that space. Buddy and Jet are going to love it."

Natalie pulled hard on her brakes and rode along beside Andi at walking pace. "I'm sure the yard is great," she sighed. "But I wish I could say the same about this hill. I'm not looking forward to riding up it again tomorrow."

Andi's feet were really starting to hurt when at last they turned onto Aspen Drive. While Natalie chained her bike up and Tristan tucked his skateboard under the porch, Andi pushed open the front door with her shoulder and hopped over the doormat as she pulled off her sneakers one by one. The tile floor was lovely and cool through her socks.

"I'm in here, honey!" Mrs. Talbot called from the living room. "Do you have Tristan and Natalie with you? There's plenty to eat if they want to stay."

Andi glanced around for Buddy.

"If you're looking for Buddy, he's upstairs in your room," her mom went on, as if she could see through the wall. "I can't get him to come downstairs."

Andi took the stairs two at a time, right to the top of the house. She pushed open the door to her attic room, with its cool, sloped ceiling. "Bud?" she called. "What's up?"

The terrier was sitting on her bed, his back to the door. He looked around at the sound of Andi's voice, but didn't jump down to greet her. He was obviously in a bad mood.

Andi sat next to him on the bed. "What have I done now, Bud?" she asked, stroking his rough tan coat. "Mom fed you, didn't she?"

Natalie and Tristan clambered into the room then. Buddy sighed and turned his back again.

"What's up with him?" Tristan asked, flopping down on one of Andi's brightly colored floor cushions.

Andi shook her head. "Beats me," she shrugged. "Come on, we'd better make this poster before supper."

Down in Mrs. Talbot's study, they crowded around the screen as Andi scanned the photograph of Raisin and dropped in the familiar Pet Finders Club logo and the usual contact details. Andi kept expecting to hear Buddy's claws clicking down the stairs, but the terrier didn't appear.

They printed out fifty posters and put them in Andi's backpack, ready to put up the next day. Andi glanced around for Buddy again. Then it hit her.

"I forgot his walk! It's six thirty already, and I always walk him way before now."

She ran upstairs to her room. Buddy heaved a sigh and put his head back between his paws. Andi went over to the bed and gave him a big hug. "I'm sorry, Bud," she said, kissing him between the ears. "I'll take you for an extra-long walk before breakfast tomorrow, okay?"

Buddy's tail thumped slowly on the quilt.

"I guess he doesn't like any variety with his routine, does he?" said Natalie.

Andi stared at her friend. Then something struck her. "That's what Mom said when I forgot to dry Buddy's feet over the weekend!" she burst out. "Routine!" She stared at the others hopefully — but they just looked confused. "What was Raisin's normal routine on a Monday? Do you think yesterday was somehow different?"

Tristan sat up. "We'd have to go back to the Harrises tonight and ask them."

But Mrs. Talbot had another idea. "You can't go out again now," she said, shaking her head when Andi asked her. "It's late, and it's dark out. The Harrises might be having their dinner, so you can't call, either. Can it wait until tomorrow?"

The kids reluctantly agreed to save their questions for the next afternoon, when they would see the Harrises after school. Andi tried not to think about the old Dalmatian, scared and shivering somewhere on the streets of Orchard Park, wondering why his owners hadn't come to find him.

She bent down and rubbed her aching toes. Even though running was one of her favorite hobbies, she was secretly glad they weren't going out again tonight.

"Dean's going to help us put up the posters," Tristan announced when they met up after school on Wednesday afternoon by the bicycle shed. "Isn't that great?"

Natalie quickly took off her helmet and shook out her ponytail. "I think I might push my bike home today," she said.

"Worried your helmet will mess up your hair, Nat?" Tristan asked innocently.

Natalie turned bright red. "I'd have to get on and off constantly to do the posters," she muttered.

Tristan nodded. "Yeah, you don't want to end up in a bush in front of Dean again."

Andi linked arms with Natalie. "Well, it's nice to have some company on the ground for a change," she said diplomatically. "With Dean's help, we'll get to the Harrises nice and early."

Raisin's cheerful black-and-white face was soon grinning from every tree, mailbox, and streetlamp from Fairfield Middle School to the corner of Natalie's street. Dean attached the final poster to Natalie's front gate with a flourish. "Gotta go," he said, checking his watch. "Hope you find the dog. He looks really cute."

"Just what I was thinking," Natalie said dreamily, watching as Dean sauntered away across the street.

"Come on," said Andi, snapping her fingers in front of Natalie's face. "Quick! Get Jet. We still have to grab Buddy, and the Harrises are expecting us at four thirty."

"And I'm starving," Tristan added unnecessarily. Andi and Natalie rolled their eyes. One of these days, something amazing would happen: Tristan would make it from one meal to the next without needing to stop for a snack.

Half an hour later, the Pet Finders Club were sitting in a neat sunroom behind the Harrises' house, watching

Buddy and Jet romp up and down the smooth green lawn.

Mr. Harris had been putting the finishing touches on Raisin's play pit when they arrived, his bright red overalls a cheerful splash of color in the gray fall afternoon. He had waved away Andi and Natalie's anxious apologies that their dogs were wrecking the play pit. "It's nice that they're enjoying it," he said sadly. "At least I know Raisin will like it." *If he ever comes home.* The thought hung uncomfortably in the air without being said out loud.

When Andi asked about Raisin's routine, Mrs. Harris smiled knowingly. "How funny you should ask that!" she exclaimed. "We did do things a little differently on Monday, because of my husband's day off."

Tristan glanced up from studying the sandwiches on the plate Mr. Harris was offering him. "So what would you normally do at five o'clock?" he asked, his hand hovering above the sandwiches.

"My regular train from the city gets in at five fifteen," Mr. Harris explained. "Mary and Raisin usually drive to meet me at the station, or walk if the weather's nice."

Andi glanced at the others. Were they thinking the same thing?

"Is it possible that Raisin went to meet you at your train as usual, Mr. Harris?" Andi asked cautiously. "It looks like he was headed in the right direction, according to the girl at the end of the street."

He set the sandwiches down, looking surprised. "I suppose so," he said. "That's clever. And just the sort of thing Raisin would do!"

"Buddy gave me a clue." Andi explained about Buddy's reactions — first to his wet paws, then his missed walk. While she was talking, she glanced through the window. Buddy was chasing Jet straight toward the play pit. Jet stretched his legs and gracefully leaped across the gap, but there was no way Buddy's little legs would clear it.

"Uh-oh," Andi said, standing up to get a better look. "I think . . . "

Flying over the edge of the pit, Buddy yelped with surprise and disappeared into the sand.

" . . . he forgot about the play pit," Andi finished. "Thanks for the tea, Mrs. Harris. The dogs really love your yard, but I think we should go check out the station now, before it gets too dark."

Clouds were beginning to roll in from the west, and the mountains looked hazy against the skyline, like it was already raining there. Andi and the others said good-bye to the Harrises and set off toward the station, following the route Raisin had taken. Natalie tried to hold Jet's leash and ride her bike at the same time, but after a couple of near misses with parked cars, she dismounted, tying Jet's leash to one of the handlebars. She and Andi walked side by side with the dogs, watching as Tristan zigzagged along the road on his skateboard, like a skier on a slope.

They slowly wound their way down the hill, across a couple of busy junctions, and up to the brightly lit station, where a train had just pulled in. Andi glanced back at the junctions and felt a stab of worry. If Raisin had really come this far, would he have crossed the road okay?

The train pulled slowly away as commuters in dark suits and overcoats spilled out of the station. Andi checked her watch. "This must be the five fifteen," she said. "Mr. Harris's usual train. I bet most of these passengers travel on this train every day. Quick, let's ask a couple of them if they saw Raisin on Monday."

They plowed into the tide of commuters, asking as many people as they could. Everyone was hurrying home, hoping to avoid the rain, and looked irritated or confused at being asked questions about a missing dog.

Andi struggled to control Buddy while asking about Raisin at the same time, and she could see that Natalie was having the same trouble.

"This is pointless," Natalie panted, unwinding Jet's leash from around her legs for about the tenth time.

"Let's ask the staff instead," Tristan suggested, as the flood of commuters slowed to a trickle.

No one in the office or along the platform could help, although the ticket clerk took the poster and agreed to put it up on the bulletin board. They asked a couple of people who were sitting in the waiting room, but they didn't recognize Raisin.

"I can't believe *no one* saw him," Tristan said in exasperation as they left the station. "I mean, correct me if I'm wrong, but Dalmatians don't usually hang around railway stations. Guys in suits, yes. Dogs with spots, no."

"You looking for a dog with spots?" A newspaper salesman in a kiosk outside the station leaned out of his booth.

Andi swung around. "Yes!" she exclaimed, showing him the poster. "Have you seen him?"

The man sucked air through his teeth as he studied the poster. "Sure, I did," he said, not sounding the least bit sure. "Monday. No — maybe last week."

"Was he on his own?" Andi pressed.

The man frowned. "I think so," he said. "But maybe he was with someone. I don't have such a good memory for stuff like that."

"You're sure it was a Dalmatian?" Natalie asked.

"Sure, I'm sure," the man nodded. "Though maybe a Labrador, or somethin' like that. Do they have spots?"

"Er, I don't think so. But thanks, anyway," Andi said gloomily, taking back the poster. This was getting them nowhere.

"Who says Raisin came to the station on Monday at all?" Tristan pointed out as Natalie unlocked her bike. "We don't know anything. We're just guessing."

"But what about Raisin's routine?" Andi protested. "It makes perfect sense that he came this way."

"Maybe he did," said Natalie ominously, shifting her grip on Jet's leash and the handlebars as she pushed her bike along the sidewalk. She glanced at the traffic speeding past them. "Maybe he just didn't get this far."

Andi swallowed. None of them could say it out loud, but they were all obviously thinking the same thing. What if Raisin had been trying to get to the station, but got hit by a car?

They trudged along the sidewalk in silence, following the red taillights toward Main Street and home. No one could think of anything to say. Andi tried to overcome her gloomy thoughts by considering the possibility that Raisin had been stolen. It seemed an odd way to cheer herself up, but it was better than thinking about him hurt — or worse. She tugged on Buddy's leash, pulling the little terrier close to her side.

"Guys!" Tristan said suddenly. Andi and Natalie looked up. "I know I've said it before, but this time, I'm really, really sure." He took a deep breath. "I just saw Lucy!"

Chapter Four

Natalie sighed and pulled her bike to a halt. "Tristan, we've been through this before," she said. "You have to stop jumping every time you see a tabby in the street."

Andi nodded. "She's right, Tristan," she said, trying to sound sympathetic because she knew how bad it felt to lose a pet. "Remember all that stuff you said outside school? Lucy's gone. I know it's hard, but — "

Tristan's eyes were blazing with excitement. "Listen," he said impatiently, cutting Andi off. "I really mean it this time, okay? Look over there. If that's not Lucy, then I swear I'll never eat another Banana Beach brownie again." He pointed across the street.

"Be careful what you promise," Andi warned him. "We'll hold you to it. You eat too many of those brownies, anyway." She turned to look where he was pointing and frowned. There were no cats on that side of the street. "Where?" she asked.

"There!" Tristan said. "On the poster!"

There was a bus shelter on the opposite side of the street, with a large poster plastered across its side. It showed a striped tabby cat sitting up on its hind legs as someone offered it a dish of food. The cat's head was tilted to one side, and its mouth was open.

"KittyKins!" the poster declared. "Your cat will love you for it! As seen on TV."

"KittyKins. Isn't that the cat food we saw at Paws for Thought on Saturday?" Andi remembered.

Tristan ran to a nearby crosswalk and jabbed hard at the button. "Come *on!*" he called. "We have to get a closer look at that poster!"

"You think Lucy's the KittyKins cat?" Natalie gasped. "Isn't that kind of unlikely?"

The lights changed, and Tristan ran across the road without answering. Andi and Natalie followed him just before the lights changed back, and found Tristan with his face pressed against the poster like he wanted to climb inside. "Lucy," he whispered. "It's you, isn't it? I'd know you anywhere."

"What makes you so sure?" Andi asked, peering closer. The cat did look like the one in Tristan's memory book. But tabby cats were like nickels and dimes. Could you really tell them apart when they were on their own?

"What makes you so sure Buddy's Buddy?" Tristan shot back.

Andi looked down at Buddy. The little terrier gazed adoringly up at her. It was true that to other people, he just looked like a regular terrier: tan and white, short legs, pricked ears, and a rough, bristly coat. But even without the unique missing claw and white-tipped ear there was something about the look in his eyes that told her she'd be able to pick Buddy out of a lineup of ten, twenty, *fifty* other Jack Russells. She'd know him anywhere, even if she hadn't seen him for months and months.

"Okay," she said eventually. "Maybe you're right. But this is crazy! How can it be Lucy on the poster?"

Jet sniffed at the poster and gave a sharp bark at the sight of such a large cat. "That cat's *famous*!" Natalie squealed, tugging on Jet's leash. "Look, it says 'as seen on TV.' Do you seriously think you own a celebrity cat?"

"Right now, I don't own a cat at all," Tristan said heavily. "Come on, we need to check this out. If I see Lucy on the commercial, I'll know for sure. We have to get to a TV. *Now!*"

*   *   *

They raced back to Aspen Drive as fast as they could. Crazy as it seemed, Tristan's excitement was infectious.

"Hey!" Andi's mom exclaimed as they burst through the front door in an explosion of dog leashes and skateboards. "Take it easy!"

"Excuse me, Mrs. Talbot!" Tristan said, rushing toward the living room. "Can I watch your TV?"

Natalie hurriedly removed her jacket and sneakers. "If he sees the commercial, he's bound to be disappointed. I mean, it can't really be Lucy. *Can* it?"

"I don't want to know," said Mrs. Talbot, shaking her head at Andi before she started explaining. "I get the feeling that it's complicated."

"It's a good story," Andi promised, easing off her sneakers. "But you're right. It is complicated."

A blister was swelling underneath her big toe. Jet sniffed her foot, and Buddy gave Andi's ankle a comforting lick. She patted them and hopped into the kitchen with the dogs padding behind her. She dug through the cupboards and drawers until she found a bandage, carefully wound it around her toe, then stood up and pressed her foot on the floor. It was still sore, but it would do.

"Mom," she began, sitting down at the table and grabbing an apple from the fruit bowl. "Do you think I could get a bike?"

Her mom made a face. "They're pretty expensive, Andi."

"My old bike was secondhand," Andi reminded her, resting her chin in her hands and giving her best puppy-dog look. "And you did say when we left it back in Florida that I could get another one, remember? It would mean I can keep up with the others more, now that Nat has a bike. All this running is ruining my feet!" She wiggled her toe at her mom, hoping the bandage would get a little sympathy.

"You can take a look," her mom conceded. "Maybe Rocky has some ads in her store window."

"Great!" Andi said happily, throwing the apple core in the trash. "Thanks!"

"Just remember that even if you do find one we can afford, Buddy will still need his walks," Mrs. Talbot warned. "He may not be able to keep up with you on a bike. He has pretty short legs."

Andi bent down and scratched Buddy between the shoulders. "As if I'd forget," she said.

Suddenly, there was a yell from across the hall. "It's her! I knew it!"

Andi flew into the living room. Tristan was kneeling in

front of the TV, which he had tuned to the local in-fomercial channel. His face was only a couple of inches from the screen. A cat-food commercial was airing, with a snappy-themed tune made up of meows and purrs set to music. Natalie was lying on the sofa, watching Tristan with a wary expression on her face.

There was the tabby cat from the poster. It was balancing on a fence, putting one foot daintily in front of the other like a model on a runway. When it reached the end of the fence, it leaped down gracefully and rubbed its head against someone's legs as they bent down with a bowl of food.

Tristan couldn't get his words out quickly enough. "Lucy used to do that! She used to walk along our fence like a circus artist. And see the way the markings are different on her left side than her right? I couldn't check that on the poster."

On screen, the cat was bending toward the bowl of KittyKins like it hadn't seen food for a week. "*Like any cat, he knows what he wants,*" declared the voiceover. "*KittyKins. Your cat will love you for it.*"

"Lucy's a *she,*" Tristan said scornfully at the screen. Then he laughed in disbelief. "Good old Lucy! A TV star! I have to get a can of KittyKins so I can prove it's her. My family is *so* not going to believe this."

Andi decided not to point out that the cat really could be a 'he' and, therefore, not Lucy at all. "Rocky's store probably has KittyKins," she said, glancing hopefully at her mom. It would be a good chance to look for second-hand bicycles in the store window, too.

"Go on then," her mom said. "Supper will be on the table in twenty minutes. Homemade pizza with extra pepperoni. If you're too late, Buddy and Jet will have something to celebrate."

Rocky Brand's convenience store was only a couple of blocks from Andi's house.

"No bicycles for sale," Andi mourned, checking Rocky's window for notices.

Natalie poked her in the ribs. "Feet not fast enough anymore? With all that training? All those laps around the soccer field?"

"Laugh all you want," Andi said. "Mom says I can have one, if I can find one that's cheap enough."

Tristan peered through the window. " 'Kiddy bike for sale,' " he read. " 'Three wheels, supersafe, with free knee pads.' There you go, Andi. Sounds perfect, and it's only twenty dollars."

"Ha-ha," said Andi, pushing open the door. "You're just afraid I'll beat you both once I get a set of wheels.

Hey, Rocky," she greeted the woman behind the counter.

Rocky returned the smile. "Hey yourself!" she replied. "How can I help you today?"

"We're looking for a cat food called KittyKins," Andi explained. "Tristan's convinced the picture on the front is his cat."

"If it's your cat, wouldn't you know about the job?" Rocky asked, sounding puzzled. "Or do you think someone's been secretly taking her picture?"

Tristan shrugged. "It's a long story. Do you have any cans?"

"Third aisle, top shelf," said Rocky. "I haven't seen you in here much lately," she said to Andi. "How's the pet-finding business?"

Andi told her about Raisin and the Harrises, and pulled a poster from her backpack for Rocky to put in her window. "We thought we'd tracked him to the station, but then we lost the trail," she said gloomily.

Rocky looked down at the poster. "I knew a dog that used to catch the train," she said. "A lovely Old English sheepdog. What was his name now?" She reflected for a moment. "Thumper! That was it. He caught the same train as me, every morning when I went to school. He was so big, he took up most of the aisle, but no one minded. On cold days, if you got a seat near him, you could warm your feet in his fur."

Andi jumped as if she'd been stung by a wasp. "Hey!" she cried excitedly. "Maybe Raisin *did* get to the station after all. But maybe he actually *caught a train!*"

"One can of KittyKins," said Tristan, triumphantly placing the can on the counter. He saw Andi and Natalie standing with their mouths open. "What's going on?"

Andi told him about her suspicion that Raisin might have boarded a train, looking for Mr. Harris.

"That's brilliant!" Tristan said admiringly. "Why didn't we think of that before?" He handed Rocky the money for the cat food. "Come on, let's grab our wheels and get back to the station!"

Andi groaned and laid her head on the counter. "I don't suppose you sell bikes, too, Rocky?" she muttered. "I only have one pair of feet and it feels like they've run across most of Orchard Park this afternoon."

Rocky bowed. "Your wish is my command," she said.

"What?" Andi stood up, startled.

"Not for sale," Rocky admitted, "but there's a bike out back if you want to borrow it. My nephew loaned it to me a while back, but I've never used it. There's a helmet, too."

Andi looked at Rocky, who was a lovely person, but who wasn't exactly young and fashion-conscious. She had a vision of an old contraption with a big basket, clunky wheels, and brown mudguards. "I'm not sure . . . " she said hesitantly.

"You wait right there, and I'll wheel it out," said Rocky, disappearing through the curtain at the back of the store. Andi's heart sank.

"It might be okay," said Tristan, who was obviously thinking the same thing. "You know, if you like antiques."

Natalie giggled and smugly swung her lilac bike helmet by its strap. But she stopped when Rocky reappeared with a bright red mountain bike. It looked brand-new and just like the most expensive models in the store where Natalie had bought her helmet. Andi stared at the bike's gleaming aluminum trim and a funky zigzag on the crossbar. A red-and-black helmet hung from the handlebars — exactly the colors Andi would have chosen for herself.

"It might be a little big," Rocky said, "but the seat's adjustable. What do you think?"

Andi touched the bell on the handlebar. It gave a soft *ting*. "It's great!" she said wonderingly. "Can I really borrow it?"

Rocky nodded happily. "No rush to return it, either. Just look after it, okay?"

"Of course! Thanks, Rocky. You're the best!"

Outside the store, Andi carefully buckled on the helmet. The bike felt a little high, but it was comfortable. She sat for a moment, getting her balance. Then she glanced mischievously at Tristan and Natalie.

"Race you!" she said, pushing down on the pedals as hard as she could.

Andi pedaled full speed up Aspen Drive, the evening air blowing cold around her neck. The smell of roasted vegetables wafted through an open window when she reached her house and made her mouth water as she carefully wheeled the mountain bike into the garage. She had time to hug Buddy, tell her mom about the bike, and wash her hands before the others came panting up to the door.

"I'll get you for this tomorrow," Tristan gasped, waving his can of KittyKins at her. "You only won because you made it to the crossing before the lights changed."

"No daredevil races, please," Mrs. Talbot warned, setting the vegetables on the table. "Rocky's been very kind to lend you her bike. You have to take good care of it, Andi."

"Did Andi tell you our latest idea about Raisin, Mrs. Talbot?" Natalie asked, helping herself to the vegetables.

Andi explained. "Tristan wants to go over to the station later tonight," she began.

Mrs. Talbot held up her hand. "Oh, no! You can call the Harrises after supper and tell them your theory, but putting it into practice will have to wait until the morning. You can't solve the case in one night, Andi, however much you want to."

Andi made the call when she and the others had finished washing up. Mrs. Harris sounded sad when she picked up. Andi outlined their new idea.

"Caught the train?" Mrs. Harris echoed in a panicky voice. "You mean he could have gone to the *city*? How will we find him there?"

"We're doing everything we can, Mrs. Harris," Andi promised. "You have my word on that."

"So, if Raisin caught the train," said Tristan when Andi had finished the call, "we should catch the train, too. Right?" He flipped a couple of grapes in the air and tipped his head back with his mouth open.

Andi reached out and caught a grape midair. "Right," she said, popping the grape into her own mouth. "How about we spend Saturday morning on the train, checking out all the stations?"

"Great idea," said Tristan. "At least we'll feel like we're doing something useful."

"What about Paws for Thought?" Natalie reminded him.

"I'll ask Christine if I can work on Saturday afternoon this weekend," Tristan decided.

"We'll take a stack of posters with us," Natalie said, getting into the idea. "We can hand them out as we go along. Poor Raisin! Do you think he's gone far?"

Mrs. Talbot was frowning. "I don't like the idea of you three riding around on a train unaccompanied," she said.

"Don't worry," Tristan said. "My dad's friend Stuart works on the trains, Mrs. Talbot. And he always works on Saturdays, so we'll make sure and catch his train. How's that?"

Mrs. Talbot smiled. "Perfect," she said. "Now all you have to do is find Raisin."

"It'll be a breeze," said Andi confidently. It really felt like they were on the right track. And Raisin was one of the most distinctive missing pets they'd ever looked for, with all those gorgeous spots. *How many places can a Dalmatian hide?* Andi thought to herself.

Chapter Five

Saturday dawned bright but bitterly cold. Andi opened her window and took a deep breath of icy air, narrowing her eyes against the sunshine. There was snow on the mountaintops in the distance, like a dusting of powdered sugar. Andi leaned her chin in her hand and stared at the view. The mountains looked close enough to touch. Smiling, she reached out her hand, just to check.

"I think we might have snow this week," her mom said when Andi clattered into the kitchen for breakfast.

"Awesome!" Andi grinned, piling her plate with toast and jelly and slopping some orange juice into a glass. "I've never seen snow." She took a thoughtful bite out of the toast-and-jelly sandwich she'd made, trying to picture what it would be like. Probably much colder than powdered sugar, but would it be soft and fluffy or wet?

"Florida didn't really do winter, did it?" her mom agreed.

The doorbell rang. "That's them," Andi said, getting up and putting her plate in the dishwasher. "Tristan's dad's friend Stuart is working on the nine twenty-six train today. He's going to wait for us at the station, so we can't be late."

"But how will you be able to question everyone along the route if you have to stay on the train?" asked Mrs. Talbot.

Andi grinned. "We're going to let the posters do the talking!" she joked, holding up her stuffed backpack. "We'll just get off long enough at each stop to put one up, then hope that people call us if they've seen Raisin."

Her mom looked worried. "Well, just make sure you get back on the train at every station," she said. "I don't want two of you coming back without the other one."

"Don't worry, Mom. Stuart will keep an eye on us. We won't do anything silly." Andi wondered briefly what they'd do if they spotted Raisin out the window somewhere along the line. *We'll deal with that when the time comes*, she decided.

Buddy was waiting for her by the door, wagging his tail. Grabbing her warmest jacket, Andi bent down to give him a pat. "Sorry, Bud," she said. "You'd hate it if

I took you on the train. Be a good boy and keep Mom company."

Outside, Tristan was so well wrapped up that Andi could hardly see his face.

"Mom made me put on about sixteen layers," he complained, pulling the scarf away from his chin. "Natalie's been teasing me the whole way about looking like a yeti."

Natalie was waiting on the sidewalk with her bike; in her silver faux-fur jacket and neat lilac-and-gray mittens to match her helmet, she looked as stylish as ever.

"Mom thinks there's going to be snow this week," said Andi, swinging her leg over her bicycle and tightening her helmet strap. "Isn't that great?"

Natalie rolled her eyes. "No," she said. "Snow is boring. It's cold and wet, and you have to shovel it away from your doorstep every morning. You didn't miss anything when you lived in Florida."

"I don't believe you," Andi argued. "I can't wait to go sledding and build snowmen and all that stuff."

She pushed hard on the pedals and the bike shot down the path. The road flew beneath her wheels with a quiet whirring sound that Andi loved. She was thrilled to have a bike, even if it was only hers for a short time. It was much faster than running, and she was still keeping fit.

There was a long hill on the way to the station, but Andi just stood up on the pedals and switched down a gear. She glanced over her shoulder. Nat was sailing serenely behind her, her nose looking a bit red in the wind, while Tristan stomped doggedly along on his skateboard, weighed down by all his clothes.

Unlike Wednesday evening, the station was almost deserted. Only a few passengers stood on the platform, stamping their feet in the cold. Andi and Natalie locked their bikes while Tristan persuaded a helpful ticket clerk to look after the helmets and the skateboard.

Andi glanced up and down the platform for someone who might be a friend of Tristan's dad. She caught sight of a red-haired man some way down the platform.

Tristan had spotted him, too. "Hey, Stu!" he bellowed, raising both arms to wave. The ginger-haired man waved back, his other hand gripping a plastic mug of coffee.

"Do you have to be so loud, Tris?" Natalie winced. "Everyone's looking at us."

"Do you want to find Raisin or not?" Tristan demanded. Natalie couldn't give him a clever reply because the man was approaching. In a funny way, with his wiry hair and small bright eyes, he reminded Andi of Buddy.

"You're looking for a dog, I hear," he said, nodding at Andi and Natalie when Tristan introduced them. "Well, best of luck. There are five stations between Orchard Park and the end of the line. You're sure this dog was headed out of town, are you? I mean, trains go both ways from this station."

Andi felt the blood drain from her face. All they knew was that Raisin had been seen heading toward the station and perhaps made it onto the concourse, if the newspaper guy's evidence could be trusted. But they had no way of knowing which way the train was going, if he even boarded one! "We don't know," she admitted. She looked desperately at the others. How could they have overlooked this major detail?

Tristan noticed Andi's expression. "We think he came to meet Mr. Harris's train, right?" he prompted. "And Mr. Harris's train was coming *from* the city. So if Raisin caught the five fifteen, he would have kept going in the same direction."

"But we can't be sure," Natalie pointed out. "It's not like he'd have seen Mr. Harris getting off the train every time, especially if Mrs. Harris ever waited for him outside the station." She looked at Stuart. "Is there a train that heads *to* the city around the same time?"

"There's a five nineteen," said Stuart.

"So Raisin *could* have caught that one and gone the other way," Natalie said, looking as worried as Andi.

Andi sat down on the hard metal bench and tried to gather her thoughts. Stuart checked his watch. "My train's due any time," he warned. "So you guys had better make a decision. If you want to go in the other direction, you'll have to wait a couple of hours until I'm coming back this way. I can't let you go into the city on your own."

Andi frantically racked her brain. In the distance, she could see the glimmering headlight of the 9:26 train. She raised her eyes to the roof of the station. She needed some serious inspiration.

"Stairs!" Tristan blurted suddenly. "Raisin hates stairs! Remember? The Harrises told us! So it's much less likely that he went to the city. The city platform is over there." He pointed triumphantly at the steep steps that went up and over the track, taking passengers to the opposite platform. "He'd never have gone up there on his own, which means if he got onto a train, it must have been from this side."

"Of course!" Natalie agreed.

"Tristan, you're a genius," said Andi in relief.

The train pulled into the station then with a noisy hiss of brakes. Stuart hopped aboard as soon as the doors slid open, somehow managing not to drop his coffee. "I have to go check in with the driver," he said, nodding to the front of the train. "Get yourselves some seats, and I'll catch up with you at the first stop."

"Did you ask Stuart if he saw Raisin on Monday?" Natalie asked Tristan, as they followed Stuart onto the train.

"Dad explained on the phone last night," said Tristan, leading the way to a vacant row of seats. "Stuart said he didn't know anything about a Dalmatian. Never mind. There's six stations out there, waiting for our posters."

Andi wriggled out of her coat and stretched out her long legs so that her feet caught a blast of warm air from the heating vents under the seats.

"What did your family think about that can of KittyKins, Tristan?" Natalie asked.

"Oh, yeah. I forgot to tell you," Tristan said, his eyes lighting up. "They think it's Lucy, too! I mean, it took a little persuading, but I convinced them in the end."

Natalie glanced at Andi and raised her eyebrows. Andi knew what she was thinking. If the cat on the can was really Lucy, surely Tristan's family wouldn't have needed *persuading*? It would be so tough if Tristan was just disappointed all over again.

"I did some research on the Internet about the pet-food manufacturers," Tristan went on, "and guess what? Their phone number has a Seattle area code! I called them, but I couldn't get an answer."

"Probably because it's Saturday," Andi guessed. "You could try again on Monday. Come on," she said, pulling a poster out of her backpack and getting to her feet. "We may as well ask the passengers if they've seen Raisin. They might have been on the Monday train."

There were only six cars and fewer than two dozen passengers. No one recognized Raisin at all. It wasn't a good start, but Andi tried not to feel too disappointed. They still had the whole line to check out. The train soon left Orchard Park behind, skimming through the vast orchards of fruit trees that gave the town its name. Andi pressed her nose to the window and watched as they headed into the country.

"The first station's coming up," Stuart warned, passing with his ticket puncher. "If you want to hop off and put up a poster or two, you'd better be quick about it. We only stop for a couple of minutes."

Looking rather nervous, Natalie volunteered to go first. The platform at Bellview had a small ticket booth and a bulletin board. As soon as the doors slid open, she shot off the train and stuck the poster on the board. Then she raced back, giggling, and flung herself onto the waiting train. "That was scary," she confessed. "Your turn next, Tristan."

The next station was called Hill Lane. It was bigger than Bellview, and there were two bulletin boards — one at each end of the platform.

"Time me," said Tristan, flexing his fingers as the train pulled into the platform. Andi watched as he raced off to pin the first poster to the farthest board.

"This is the nine forty-three for Oakwood," the announcer droned. "All aboard, please! All aboard!"

Tristan skidded and almost fell over as he raced toward the second bulletin board. The doors gave a gentle ringing sound.

"Come on!" Natalie shrieked, jumping up and down. "The doors are about to close!"

Tristan made it with just inches to spare, the doors grazing the back of his jacket. "How fast was I?" he panted.

"One minute and twenty-two seconds," Andi said. "Not bad, but I bet I can do better at the next stop." She glanced back at the platform as the train pulled away and wondered if anyone would look at Raisin's poster close enough to recognize him.

At Durham, Andi ran so fast up the platform that she made enough time for a few words with the station

guard before getting back on the train. "He said he'd have remembered a Dalmatian," she told the others breathlessly, "because he has one himself. So it doesn't look like Raisin got off here."

Natalie managed to drop her poster between the train and the platform at Rivertown, the next station along the line, and Tristan only had time to thrust a poster at the station guard at Pine Junction. They were almost at the end of the line.

Settling back in her seat, Andi stared at the view. They were deep in farm country now. Tall pine trees lined the railway track, and between the tree trunks she glimpsed wide-open fields and the glint of a river.

"Oakwood! This is Oakwood!" came the announcer's voice.

They got off the train. Andi shivered as the cold wind cut through her coat, and she pulled her scarf tighter around her neck. The air felt even sharper out here than back home.

Stuart disappeared into the staff room to grab another cup of coffee. "Keeps my fingers warm," he said with a grin when he returned. "So, any luck on this missing Alsatian so far?"

"Alsatian?" Andi repeated with a frown. "Raisin's a *Dalmatian*."

She pulled out a poster and thrust it under Stuart's nose. Stuart's mouth dropped open. "A Dalmatian?" he said. "I could have sworn your dad said it was an Alsatian, Tris."

"Dad's not great on details." Tristan rolled his eyes. "Unless you're talking central heating, power showers, or hardwood flooring."

Stuart took a sip of his coffee. "Maybe I just heard wrong," he said. "Well, if it's a Dalmatian you're looking for, I might be able to help after all. A pal of mine mentioned that he'd seen a big, spotted dog on his train."

Andi and Natalie both gasped and Tristan clutched at Stuart's arm, almost knocking the cup out of his hand.

"Hey!" Stuart protested. "Watch the coffee, okay?"

"When was this?" Andi demanded.

"I don't know the time exactly," Stuart confessed, "but I think it was Monday. He told me about some kid on his train who was hollering. Apparently, this dog had helped himself to the kid's snack."

"I bet the snack was raisins!" Natalie burst out.

"This is great," Andi enthused, forgetting about the cold seeping through the soles of her sneakers. "It looks like our hunch was right all along!"

"How do we know where he got off, though?" Tristan asked.

Andi checked that she had her cell phone turned on. "Well, there are posters pretty much all along the line between here and Orchard Park, so someone might recognize Raisin and call," she said. "In the meantime, we can start asking questions around here."

"Let's start with that porter," Natalie suggested.

But the porter couldn't help. "Why don't you try Ahmed?" he said, pointing inside the station. "He's in the ticket office today. He's crazy about dogs. If anyone saw a Dalmatian on Monday, it would be him."

At last, the Pet Finders Club struck gold.

"I remember him well!" the guard in the ticket office exclaimed when Andi showed him the poster. "He was such a beautiful dog, I couldn't miss him. I have terriers at home."

"Jack Russells?" Andi asked, forgetting about Raisin for a moment. "They're great, aren't they?"

"Do you remember if the dog was with anybody?" interrupted Tristan loudly, frowning at Andi.

The guard nodded. "Oh, yes," he said. "I would have caught him if he'd been on his own. He was with a lady. I remember. A lady with brown hair."

"Someone on the Monday train saw Raisin with a kid," Natalie said. "Did the woman have a child with her?"

"No, not that I recall." The guard frowned, trying to remember. "I think she was wearing overalls and boots. You know, like she worked on a farm."

Andi glanced around the station. Almost every person on the concourse had the wind-roughened faces and battered outdoor clothes of farmers and outdoor workers. She sighed. It looked like their luck just ran out — again.

Chapter Six

"It'll be like looking for an apple in an orchard," Natalie groaned as they stood in a huddle outside the station.

"At least we know it's a woman," said Andi, trying to look on the bright side. "You know, that could cut out about fifty percent of the Oakwood population."

Tristan glanced up at a billboard over their heads. It was advertising a local hay and feed merchant. "Check out that area code!" he gasped. "Talk about weird!"

Andi glanced at it. It was just an ordinary Seattle code.

"Yeah, it's got numbers and everything!" Natalie said sarcastically.

Tristan gave her a withering look. "Not that you're interested," he said, "but it's the same code as the Kitty-Kins manufacturer. They must be based around here!"

"Hey!" Stuart came running out of the station, still

holding his coffee. "I thought I'd lost you there for a moment. We're turning around in one hour, so you have to be back here by ten after eleven or you'll miss the train. I can't wait around, and I don't want to explain to your folks that you guys are missing in Oakwood. Got it?"

Andi checked her watch. It was a quarter after ten. "We'll be back by eleven," she promised. "We'll just head for the main street, put up a few posters, and ask a couple of questions. You never know. That clue about Raisin with the lady in overalls might help."

Stuart nodded. "Good luck with the hunt!" he said. "See you in an hour."

"Where do you think the KittyKins manufacturer could be?" Tristan asked, scanning the streets as they walked toward town.

"Why?" Andi said jokingly, handing him a stack of posters. "Are you thinking of breaking in?"

Tristan's eyes gleamed.

"Oh, no," Natalie said, shaking her head. "We're not going there."

Tristan stepped up his pace. "Right, it's *only* my long-lost cat," he said sulkily. "That doesn't matter, I guess."

Andi held up her hand, trying to keep the peace. "No one said Lucy wasn't important, Tristan," she said. "It's just that we need to focus on Raisin right now."

Tristan kicked moodily at an old can that was lying on the sidewalk, but he didn't say anything else.

"Come on," said Andi, digging in her backpack for a handful of posters. "Let's put some of these up."

Natalie pulled string and tape from her bag, and they moved down the main street, carefully putting up posters of Raisin on trees and fences and asking if they could leave posters in Oakwood's store windows. Several people stopped and asked what they were doing. Whenever someone expressed an interest in the posters, Andi made sure to ask them if they'd seen Raisin with a brown-haired woman in overalls. But although everyone was willing to help, no one had seen a woman like that with a Dalmatian.

The last stop they made was the local police station. The officer on duty put their poster up on the board beside the reception desk and listened sympathetically to Andi's description of the lady in overalls. "That describes most folks in this town," he said, shaking his head. "There's a lot of farming folk around here. But we'll give you a call if someone tells us they picked up a lost dog."

Back outside, the wind was picking up, swirling dead leaves around Andi's ankles and making her acutely aware of her thin cotton socks.

"It's five to eleven, guys," she said, stamping her feet to keep the blood flowing to her toes. "It doesn't look like we're going to find Raisin or the overalls lady today. We'll just have to hope she sees the poster and calls us. We should head for the train. We told Stuart we'd be back by eleven."

"Good," Natalie said, rubbing her hands together. "My fingers are about to fall off."

Andi looked up at the sky, which had a faint yellowish cast. Her heart gave a little skip. "Is that what it looks like when it's going to snow?" she asked hopefully.

"Yup," said Tristan. "I hope it holds out until we get home."

With their heads tucked into their collars, they walked away from Oakwood's small main street toward the station.

Halfway there, Tristan darted down a side street.

"Hey!" Andi called in surprise. "Where are you going?"

"It'll just be a minute," Tristan called over his shoulder, breaking into a jog. "I thought I saw — Aha!"

He pointed triumphantly at a four-story, steel-gray building behind padlocked gates. The windows were dark and lifeless, and there was barbed wire along the top of the perimeter fence. Large pink letters spelled KITTYKINS across the top story of the building.

Andi couldn't believe her eyes. Just a few moments ago, she'd thought Tristan was crazy to think that in the miles and miles covered by one area code, they would stumble across the very building he was determined to find. One thing was for sure — if it really *was* Lucy in the KittyKins ads, Tristan was definitely meant to find her.

"It's closed," Natalie said unnecessarily.

Tristan made a tutting sound. "I know it's closed," he said, sounding impatient. "I just want to take a look."

"We don't have time," Andi objected, looking toward the station. It was past eleven, and the station was still some way off.

Tristan ignored her and ran toward the KittyKins building. Andi and Natalie had no choice but to follow. When they reached him, Tristan was peering through the padlocked gate. "There's a huge picture of Lucy outside the main door!" he said in delight.

"I'm sure Lucy doesn't live at the factory," Andi said, trying to pull him away. "She'd probably live with someone who looks after show-business animals. We're going to miss the train, Tris. Come on."

Tristan muttered with frustration, craning his head to look back at the building as Andi and Natalie towed him toward the street.

"It's five after eleven already," Andi said anxiously, let-

ting go of Tristan's arm and starting to run. "We have to hurry or Stuart will leave without us!"

"I just want to find Lucy," Tristan muttered, shoving his hands deep into his pockets.

"I know," Natalie soothed, pushing him along. "We all do. But right now, we have to run!"

There was a shuddering noise from the station. Andi ran faster. "Get a move on!" she yelled over her shoulder. "They've started the engine."

She sprinted the last hundred yards, enjoying the feeling of warmth in her arms and legs as her muscles buzzed into action. Passengers were getting onto the train, and the announcer was halfway through his list of destinations.

"I thought you'd never make it!" Stuart reached out a hand to help Andi into the car. "Where are the others?"

"This is the eleven ten for Seattle, stopping at Pine Junction, Rivertown . . . " the announcer droned.

Tristan and Natalie tore around the corner and leaped onto the train, reaching out their hands so Andi could pull them aboard. Out of breath, they collapsed onto one of the seats. The doors made their familiar ringing sound just as the guard who had told them about the woman in overalls came running up the platform.

"I remembered something else!" he called, waving at

them. "The lady in overalls had a bag with her, with a picture of a piece of cheese on it."

There was a hiss and the doors started to slide shut, but he continued. "There's a market in town on Thursdays!" he shouted through the rapidly closing gap. "I thought maybe she worked at a dairy booth — "

There was no more time. With a squeal of brakes being released, the train pulled out of Oakwood and started back toward Orchard Park. Andi smiled and quickly waved out the window to the guard, to let him know she'd heard him and appreciated the info.

"A real clue at last!" Natalie exclaimed, pulling off her hat. "We have to come back to Oakwood on Thursday, guys."

"Uh, haven't you forgotten a little something called school?" Andi inquired.

Natalie looked crestfallen. "*School*," she said, like she'd smelled something bad. "Trust school to get in the way."

Tristan was kneeling on the seats with his nose pressed to the window, watching as Oakwood slipped from view behind the pine trees. Staring at his back, Andi was suddenly worried. The whole KittyKins thing was getting way out of control.

"Tristan?" she asked, as gently as she could. "Has your family thought of maybe getting a kitten? Do you remember how Mrs. Giacomo said we could have one of Lola's?"

"I have Lucy," Tristan replied, staring out of the window. "Why would I want a kitten? I'm going to call KittyKins first thing on Monday morning. They'll tell me about the commercial. Then I can go to the TV studios."

Andi glanced at Natalie.

"It's not as easy as that," Natalie began.

Tristan swung around and glared at her. "You don't believe it's Lucy, do you?" he challenged. "You're just pretending, to make me feel better. So are you, Andi. No one believes me. Well, I'll prove it to you. Just wait and see!"

They spent the rest of the journey in silence. Andi stared at the low yellow clouds in the sky and decided they looked the way she was feeling — strange and heavy with gloom. Suddenly, snow didn't seem so exciting after all.

They got back to Orchard Park around noon. Andi and Natalie followed Tristan off the train and hung around miserably while he got his skateboard and their bike helmets from the office.

Tristan looked at them. "Enough silence," he said, with a glimmer of his old humor. "Let's just think positively about finding Lucy, okay? I know I could be wrong, but I have to find out for sure. Come on, I'll buy us a hot chocolate at the Banana Beach Café."

The brightly painted walls and rainbow awning of the Banana Beach Café cheered Andi up on the spot, as did her spicy chicken sandwich. Her mood lifted as she realized that finding Lucy was actually beginning to seem possible and finding Raisin felt almost guaranteed.

Natalie patted her lips with a napkin. "So, let's go through our Raisin clues," she said. She started checking off the clues on her fingers. "The Oakwood guard saw Raisin getting off the train with a lady in overalls. The guard later remembered that the lady was carrying a bag with a piece of cheese on it."

"A *picture* of a piece of cheese," Tristan corrected.

Natalie rolled her eyes. "It's hardly going to be a real piece of cheese, is it?"

"So we'll find our next clue at the dairy booths at the Thursday market," Andi finished.

"*We* won't find anything, thanks to school," Natalie said wryly. "It'll have to be the Harrises."

"I'll call them later," Andi promised. "Come on, Tristan, it's nearly two o'clock. If you're late, Christine will never let you swap your hours again."

"How was your morning?" Christine greeted them as they came into the pet store.

"Not bad," said Andi, and she told Christine about their new clues.

"I went to the KittyKins office in Oakwood, too," Tristan added. "But it was closed. All I want to do is *talk* to somebody about Lucy. It's so frustrating."

"If you want to talk to someone at KittyKins, you should have asked me!" Christine exclaimed. "I have a number you can call. KittyKins has a twenty-four-hour order line that's open on Saturdays."

Tristan's jaw was somewhere on the floor. "A phone number?" he stammered. "For KittyKins?"

Christine laughed at his expression. "It's a small company, so I'm sure someone will be able to help," she said, picking up the phone and dialing a number. "Maybe they'll have the number for the marketing department. Those are the people you want to speak to about the pet food commercials."

"I don't believe it!" Tristan gasped five minutes later when Christine wrote down a number and handed it to him. "This is a personal cell phone number."

Christine grinned. "No point getting an office number on a Saturday, is there? They've always been a friendly company to deal with," she said. "Go on, give them a call."

Andi gave Tristan a friendly punch on the arm. "Christine's going to work you really hard today in exchange for this information, Tris," she joked. "Are you up to it?"

Christine leaned over the counter. "There'll be no extra sweeping or extra hours," she said. "Let's just say that if that cat does turn out to be Lucy, you can bring her into the store for a celebrity event and help me sell plenty of KittyKins!"

If. The word rolled around in Andi's head, heavy with unknowable things. *If, if, if.* She wanted the KittyKins cat to be Lucy so much. How would Tristan cope with the disappointment if it wasn't?

Chapter Seven

Buddy was delighted to see Andi when she got home later that afternoon. She made a huge fuss over him, scratching him behind the ears and down his legs until his back leg kicked with delight. Then she and her mom took him for a run in the park.

Andi confided her worries about Lucy to her mom as they jogged after Buddy, who was running in circles as though straight lines were simply too dull for him. "Tabby cats aren't exactly unusual, and it's been months since Tristan has seen Lucy," she said unhappily. "Then there's the guy on the commercial calling Lucy 'he.' That's a pretty obvious mistake, isn't it? So, what if it isn't a mistake?"

"The best thing you can do for Tristan is cheer him on when he needs it," her mom advised. "And it looks like you're doing that already. You're a good friend, Andi. Tristan's lucky to have you."

Buddy pelted past them in pursuit of a duck, who didn't seem to realize it would be easier to fly than run.

"We'd better take Bud home," Mrs. Talbot said, a bit out of breath. "Before he gives that duck a heart attack."

Andi grinned sideways at her. "Nothing to do with you being tired?" she teased before speeding up toward the gate.

The first thing Andi noticed when she woke up the following morning was an eerie silence. Yawning, she pulled back the drapes.

The street outside had vanished beneath a smooth, shining blanket of white. Rooftops, cars, and fence posts had grown white hats during the night, and the sharp edges of curbs and trimmed hedges had softened and blurred together. The sky was completely clear and blue, as if the snow had somehow grown up through the ground and not fallen from clouds at all.

Andi charged downstairs. "Snow!" she whooped. "Mom, it snowed!"

Buddy leaped out of his bed in the kitchen, catching Andi's mood of excitement. She flung open the back door and ran into the yard, feeling the snow crunch under her bare feet. It was wet — not fluffy at all! And it was so cold that her toes curled up in protest. Buddy gave a yelp of surprise at the unfamiliar backyard, then tucked his tail between his legs and fled back inside.

"Andi!" Her mom appeared at the back door. "Put some clothes on, or you'll freeze to death!"

Andi rushed inside and found her warmest clothes, mittens, a hat, and a winter coat. She grabbed her boots and tugged them on, hopping toward the back door.

"It's only snow, Buddy," she said, coaxing the little dog out from beneath the kitchen table. "Come on!"

Buddy sniffed warily around the edges of the yard, seeking familiar smells. Andi flung herself down and flapped her arms, making her first-ever snow angel. Then she rolled a couple of snowballs and weighed them experimentally in her hand. *"White Christmas," eat your heart out!* she thought gleefully, taking aim and smacking a snowball straight against the back door, where it disintegrated in a shower of white.

Her mom tapped at the kitchen window and opened it a crack to call to her. "Tristan's on the phone," she called. "He wants to meet at the park in half an hour. Should I say you're doing homework?"

"Ha-ha!" Andi grinned and pushed back her hat, which was slipping over her eyes. "Half an hour? Tell him I'll see him there in fifteen minutes!"

The sun was shining, already giving the snow a wet, melted sheen. Andi jumped along the sidewalk for a while, then hopped, then tried running backward, all the time leaving a trail of footprints. Buddy's paws made a dashing line of black marks, his pads and claws clearly defined on the ground, even his tiny missing claw.

Arriving breathless at the park, Andi didn't see the snowball until it was too late. *Thud!* Something heavy slammed against her back, nearly knocking her off her feet.

"Slow reaction, Andi! Maybe we found an outdoor activity you're not great at," Tristan teased her as she brushed the snow off her shoulder and spun around. "Just because you're from Florida doesn't mean we'll give you an easy ride!" he continued.

Andi's eyes sparkled. "I don't need an easy ride!" she said. She scooped up a handful of snow and flung it as hard as she could, laughing when it caught Tristan on the side of his hat.

Natalie came hurrying into the park in her furry silver jacket and a vivid red hat, with Jet at her heels. "You are

such *babies*," she said disapprovingly. "We've got pets to find, remember? *Ouch!*" A snowball thumped her on the shoulder. "Tristan, you are totally *dead!*"

The morning flew by, filled with snowman building — and then knocking-down — more snowball fights, and some fantastic sled races on plastic bags Tristan had brought with him. After a couple of hours, Andi was breathless and soaking wet.

"I thought you said snow was boring," she reminded Natalie as they rounded up Buddy and Jet. The snow was seeping away in the bright sun now, and slushy puddles lay on the ground around the swings.

"Okay, I lied." Natalie grinned. "Hey, do you guys want to come back to my place for lunch?"

"If your mom cooks like Dean, I'll pass," Andi joked.

Natalie looked awkward. "My mom doesn't really cook much," she said. "But Maria does a mean Chicken Salsa."

Natalie's parents lived in a large house with staff and more bathrooms than an average hotel, but it wasn't something she made a big deal about. In fact, she was always a bit shy that she had more stuff than most other people. That was one of the reasons Andi liked her so much.

It was only a ten-minute walk from the park to

Natalie's house. As she followed Tristan and Natalie up the path to the imposing front steps, topped with columns as white as the snow on the lawn, Andi was suddenly aware of her wet jeans and baggy old winter coat. All the snow still hadn't washed off the trail of paw prints Buddy had left on her coat the other day.

A young woman with her hair pulled back in a braid, in a crisp white apron, stood at the door. "Come in," she said in a softly accented voice. "Lunch will be ready in ten minutes, Natalie. Your mother and Mr. Peters are in the living room."

Andi pulled off her boots and wriggled out of her coat, reddening with embarrassment as the maid took them like they were from a classy boutique. "What about Buddy?" she whispered to Natalie.

"You don't have to whisper, Andi," Natalie said impatiently. "Look, here's a towel. We'll give the dogs a rubdown, and they can go in there." She pointed to a little room by the front door. "There's a heater in there and a couple of dog beds. It's nice and warm."

Andi tugged at her sweater, wishing it was long enough to cover the mud and water stains on her jeans. Natalie somehow still looked immaculate, even after all the snow fights and sled races. Glancing at Tristan, Andi felt a little better. His red hair was standing on end after being crammed inside his hat, and he had a tear in his T-shirt sleeve.

"Let's go find some pretzels," said Natalie, heading for the kitchen. "I'm starving."

After a bowl of pretzels and a large, warm cup of tea, Andi was feeling more relaxed.

"Chicken Salsa!" Natalie's stepdad came into the kitchen, sniffing appreciatively. "Hi, guys. Have a good time in the snow?"

Mr. Peters was tall and tan, with very white teeth and friendly wrinkles around his eyes. He was wearing a pale blue cashmere sweater draped casually across his shoulders, and a gold watch gleamed on his wrist.

Natalie's mom came into the kitchen after her husband, smiling at Andi and Tristan. "Don't spoil your appetite with those pretzels, honey," she told Natalie before reaching a perfectly manicured hand into the bowl and extracting a single pretzel. Andi was a little in awe of Mrs. Peters, who never had a hair out of place and always smelled of glamorous perfume and hair products.

During lunch, Natalie told her parents about the Pet Finders' latest project.

"I love Dalmatians!" Mrs. Peters exclaimed. "They're

so chic with their spots. And you think this lady who has Raisin sells cheese?"

"We hope so," Andi said, "otherwise we're quickly running out of clues." She knew it was just as likely that the lady had picked up the bag when she bought some cheese, but Raisin's trail was getting colder every day, and they had to follow it wherever they could.

"And how are you doing on your cat hunt, Tristan?" asked Mr. Peters. "Natalie told us about it last night."

Tristan's mouth was full of chicken. He chewed frantically, unable to speak. "He called the pet food company yesterday," Andi said, helping him out. "They gave him a number for Gold TV. They make the commercials, so he's calling them tomorrow." She crossed her fingers under the table and tried to remember what her mom said about being supportive of Tristan. Would a TV company really give out information about the KittyKins commercial to a couple of kids?

"Oh, yes! Solomon Goldman — he's the owner of Gold TV. He plays tennis at my club," Mr. Peters said casually.

Tristan choked on his chicken, and Andi had to bang him on the back.

"Hey!" she exclaimed, as a fantastic idea struck her. "Do you ever need ball boys — or girls — Mr. Peters?"

"Sometimes," said Mr. Peters. "Why? Are you offering?"

"I used to help out at my mom's club in Florida in the summer," Andi said eagerly. "Buddy was really good at retrieving the balls when they went over the fence. You could use us next time you play Mr. Goldman!"

Mr. Peters raised his eyebrows. "And you can get an introduction and find out about Tristan's cat, right?" he said. Andi blushed. She hadn't realized Natalie's stepdad would see through her offer quite so quickly. But to her relief he smiled. "Smart thinking. Sol and I usually knock a couple of balls around on Sundays. The club has indoor courts — thank goodness, with all this snow. Are you free tonight around six?"

Green Lawn Tennis Club was situated on the edge of Orchard Park, tucked at the end of a winding drive and screened from the road by a row of tall pine trees. Andi and Tristan walked slowly through the gates, staring around at the landscaped grounds dotted with melting snow. A row of expensive cars was parked by the main door.

Tristan pointed at a pale gold Mercedes with the license plate GOLD 1. "I bet that's Mr. Goldman's car!" he whispered. "By the way, Andi, that was a stroke of genius asking Mr. Peters about coming to the club."

Andi grinned. "You should be thanking Mr. Peters, not me," she pointed out, hefting her gym bag over her shoulder and pushing open the reception door.

Inside, the club smelled of new carpet and fresh flowers. A blond girl glanced up from behind a sleek desk of pale wood as Andi and Tristan came in. Natalie jumped up from a low leather armchair where she'd been waiting, reading a magazine.

"My stepdad's gone in to change," she explained. "We have to pick up our uniforms at the desk and meet him on Court Three."

"Uniforms?" Andi stared as the reception girl handed them three ball-boy outfits in green and red, and a pamphlet with a map of the courts and the rules of the club. "We didn't have uniforms in Florida."

Tristan admired the T-shirt, shorts, and green cap with GREEN LAWN TENNIS CLUB printed in red. "Can we take them home afterward?" he asked hopefully.

"Sure," said Natalie, holding the uniform up and wrinkling her nose in disgust. "If you have twenty-five dollars and, like, zero taste. Otherwise you have to leave them in the laundry. Do I really have to wear this?" she asked the receptionist. "The color is awful under these fluorescent lights."

The receptionist shrugged.

"Oh, well," Natalie said gloomily, draping the uniform over her arm. "This had better be worth it, is all I can say."

Mr. Goldman was a small, wiry man with a shock of black hair, who hit the ball so hard it was little more than a yellow blur as it whizzed around the court. Andi scurried along the net to pick up the balls between points, while Natalie stood at her stepdad's end of the court and Tristan stood at Mr. Goldman's.

For all her complaining, Natalie looked like a total professional, bouncing the balls at Mr. Peters whenever he served. Tristan, on the other hand, treated it like a Saturday ball game. He kept whooping between points and couldn't resist a handstand when Mr. Goldman won a difficult tiebreaker. It was a tough game, but Mr. Goldman won the last set with only a couple of points to spare.

Victory had put Mr. Goldman in a very good mood. "So," he said, smiling broadly at Andi and the others as he wiped his forehead on a dark green towel. "You guys like TV commercials, I hear."

"We love commercials with *animals*, Mr. Goldman," Tristan said eagerly, following him along the corridor toward the changing rooms. On the way there, they'd agreed not to go into too much detail about Lucy. It was just too complicated. "You make pet food commercials, don't you?"

"Sure. We've just handled a big campaign for a local company, and they're about to start shooting again," Mr. Goldman said. "You should come along to the studio sometime."

"Why don't you give your assistant a call, Sol?" Mr. Peters put in. "She could give the kids a deluxe tour."

"Great idea!" Mr. Goldman exclaimed. "I'll call and make arrangements. How does Tuesday after school sound?"

Andi had to bite her tongue to keep herself from shouting out loud. At last, something was going right!

"Sounds perfect!" Tristan said honestly, answering for all of them. "Totally perfect."

CHAPTER EIGHT

It was dark and cold when they came out of the club. Andi pulled her hat down so that it covered more of her hair and dug her hands deep in the fleecy pockets of her running pants.

They said good-bye to Mr. Goldman and watched him drive away in a dark blue SUV, not, to Tristan's disappointment, the gold Mercedes with the personalized license plate.

"Thanks for the lift," said Andi as Mr. Peters unlocked his car and held open the door.

"And thanks for losing, Geoff," said Natalie happily, wriggling along the pale cream leather seat in the back of Mr. Peters's black Chrysler.

"You make it sound like I lost on purpose," her stepdad protested, flipping on the headlights and starting the engine.

"Did you?" Andi asked. She couldn't imagine losing anything on purpose.

Mr. Peters laughed and wouldn't answer. Jazz music was seeping into the back of the car, making Andi feel sleepy and comfortable. She rested her head on the soft leather headrest and closed her eyes.

"I can't believe we're going on a tour of Gold TV's studios on Tuesday!" Tristan said. "I bet the local company he mentioned is KittyKins, so Lucy is sure to be there. I can't believe I'm going to see her again, after all this time!"

Andi didn't point out that Tristan's last bet — on Mr. Goldman's car — hadn't worked out. *Stop being negative*, she told herself fiercely.

"You were pretty good out there tonight, Nat," she said, turning to her friend. "Where did you learn that straight-arm, legs-apart stance? Anyone would think you were a professional!" She was genuinely curious, because everyone knew Natalie wasn't into sports.

"I watched Wimbledon this summer," Natalie said simply, flipping her blond hair over her shoulder. "Not for the tennis," she added, catching Andi's disbelieving look. "To watch the players. That Argentinian guy is the cutest thing ever!"

*　*　*

It was pretty late when Andi got home. Her mom made her a quick tomato omelet, and Andi scraped the plate clean, in between giving her a full account of the evening. Buddy sat beside her, resting his head on her feet.

"You'd better go on up to bed," her mom said as she cleared the table. "School tomorrow."

Andi suddenly remembered something. "I forgot to call the Harrises! I meant to call them this afternoon and tell them about Raisin and the cheese lady, but with the excitement of the tennis game, and Lucy, and every-thing, I forgot. And I have to tell them about Thursday!"

"What about Thursday?" asked her mom.

Andi explained about the market in Oakwood. "We'd normally follow up on a clue like that, but we can't get out of school. If the Harrises don't go instead of us, they'll have to wait another whole week before finding Raisin," she groaned. "Is it too late to call?"

Mrs. Talbot gave Andi a little shove toward the stairs. "I'm sure the Harrises will be happy to go to Oakwood," she said. "Raisin is their dog, after all. Don't worry about it, Andi. You've done a great job this weekend. The Harrises will be delighted to hear all about it — tomorrow."

*   *   *

When Andi woke up on Monday morning, the snow had melted. The street looked gray and brown again, just a little bit wetter than normal. *There was something dreamlike about it*, she thought as she got ready for school, almost as if it hadn't happened at all.

She changed her mind when she got to her homeroom.

"Quiet down, please," said Mr. Dixon, Andi and Natalie's science and art teacher, rapping on his desk with a ruler. "I have good news and bad news. Which would you like to hear first?"

"The bad news," someone piped from the back of the room.

"Get it over with," Natalie muttered to Andi.

Mr. Dixon started walking between the desks, handing out papers. "Okay. The bad news is that you guys have one week to complete the following assignment," he said, amid loud groans. "You can work in pairs or groups. You can use any resources you can find at home or in the town library, and it must be handed in a week from today."

"What's the good news?" Andi asked, taking the paper from Mr. Dixon's outstretched hand and reading the title of the assignment: WHATEVER THE WEATHER: ONE HUNDRED YEARS OF NATURAL DISASTERS IN ORCHARD PARK.

Mr. Dixon handed the assignment to the last student. "This weekend's freezing weather and sudden thaw have burst a local water main," he said with a grin. "This means that the school will close for a week for emergency repairs. So, I'll see you all on Monday!"

Andi stared at her friend in disbelief. "Do you realize what this *really* means, Nat?" she asked in excitement, as they headed outside in a stream of laughing, jostling kids.

"It means we have to write a seriously boring assignment," Natalie groaned.

Andi's eyes were bright as she and Natalie unlocked their bicycles. "No! It means that we can go to Oakwood on Thursday! The assignment will be no problem. We can go to the library today and tomorrow and check the local history section for accounts of freaky weather in the past hundred years. Then we can write it on Wednesday. By Thursday, we'll be all set!"

"This is shaping up to be a great week," Tristan agreed enthusiastically, rolling up on his skateboard. "Lucy on Tuesday and Raisin on Thursday. By Saturday, we'll be ready for a whole new case."

Andi's cell phone started ringing with a cheerful thumping tune. She fumbled around in her backpack and pulled it out. "Hello?" she said.

"Is this the Pet Finders Club?" asked a man's voice on the other end.

"Yes," Andi replied.

"I've found your Dalmatian," said the man.

Andi nearly dropped the phone. "Really?" she squeaked, making frantic waving motions at the others. "Where did you find him?"

"In Oakwood," said the man. "Is there a reward?"

"Oh, I don't think so," said Andi. "But this is so great! We were all set to come find you at your cheese booth on Thursday!"

There was a pause. "Yeah," said the man finally. "But look, if you send me money for the train fare and the dog food, I'll bring him to you. No point in you coming out here."

"Oh, I guess that's an idea. Can I take your number and call you back?" asked Andi, regaining control of her voice. She covered the receiver and hissed at Tristan to get a pen out of his backpack. "I'll speak to the owners, and we'll work something out, okay?"

The man gave her his cell phone number and hung up. Andi put the phone back in her backpack and beamed at the others. "Looks like our posters have found Raisin," she said triumphantly. "The Pet Finders Club *rocks*!"

"What did she say?" Tristan wanted to know.

"It wasn't a woman, it was a man," said Andi, buckling her helmet.

Tristan looked surprised. "It wasn't the cheese lady?"

"It must have been her husband," Andi replied with a shrug. "Listen, let's call our parents and tell them about school being closed. We have to go see the Harrises right now!"

Somehow, the hill to the Harrises' house didn't seem nearly as steep as it had the previous week. Even Natalie managed to keep up, though she was huffing and puffing and pink in the face by the time they reached the Harrises' front door. Tristan brought up the rear. Andi was surprised to see that he was carrying his skateboard under his arm and had a strange, thoughtful expression on his face.

Mrs. Harris opened the door. She looked pale and sad but managed a smile when she saw who it was. Without wasting a minute, Andi told her the good news.

"That's just wonderful!" Mrs. Harris was beaming when Andi finished. Her eyes looked a little damp. "Call that man back and tell him we'll overnight him the fare at once and a little extra for his trouble."

Andi noticed that the frown on Tristan's face had

deepened. She looked hard at him, but he wouldn't meet her gaze.

"If he gets the money in tomorrow's mail, he can bring Raisin back as soon as tomorrow afternoon!" Mrs. Harris finished happily. She took out a checkbook and wrote out a large sum, leaving the space for a name blank.

"Are you sure, Mrs. Harris?" Andi asked, looking at the check. It seemed like a lot.

"Of course I'm sure," Mrs. Harris insisted. "Raisin is much more precious to us than money. Call him back and let's make the arrangements!"

"Wait." Tristan put his hand over Andi's cell as she prepared to make the call. He looked more serious than Andi had ever seen him. "I've been thinking. What's stopping anyone at all from seeing the posters and calling us to say they've found Raisin — whether they have or haven't?"

Natalie looked upset. "Why would someone do that?"

"For money," Andi said slowly. She felt sick as she saw exactly how easy it would be for a con man to pull a stunt like that. "He did ask about a reward, now that I think of it."

"And what's keeping him from just taking Mrs. Harris's check and then disappearing?" Tristan added.

Mrs. Harris's chin trembled. She'd felt so close to getting her beloved dog back. Now it looked as if she might start crying again.

"Mrs. Harris?" Andi said as gently as she could. "Is there any way we can check that this man has Raisin? Does Raisin have something special about him, something which only he has? Like, my dog Buddy has a missing claw."

Mrs. Harris sniffed, then thought. "Raisin has a funny spot that's exactly the same shape as a mushroom near his tail," she said after a minute. "Maybe you can ask him about that."

Tristan took the phone. He looked very determined as he dialed the number. "Hello? This is the Pet Finders Club, returning your call," he said. Andi and Natalie crowded in close to listen. "It's great you've found Raisin. He's such a cool dog, isn't he?"

"He's great!" the man agreed enthusiastically — a little too enthusiastically, Andi thought. "Though he's kind of expensive to feed, you know?"

He was trying to get them to send a nice, fat check, Andi realized, with a sour taste in her mouth. She was suddenly one hundred percent sure that the caller didn't have Raisin at all.

"He's real bouncy, isn't he?" Tristan was saying. "And

those spots! Have you seen that one by his tail that looks like a banana?"

"The banana!" said the man. "I noticed that today! Cute, huh?"

"No, wait," said Tristan, "it's kind of more like a . . . a . . . seashell."

"Yeah, it could be a banana-type seashell," the man replied. "Listen, when can I get the money?"

"Never," Tristan said calmly. Andi was very impressed. He sounded like an adult! "We know you're lying. We know you don't have our dog. And we have your number. So don't ever try this again, or we'll call the police."

There was silence on the other end of the phone. Andi held her breath.

"Wise guy," the man's voice snarled. "It's your loss."

Tristan held the receiver away from his ear as the caller slammed down the phone.

"Way to go, Tristan!" Natalie cheered, pounding Tristan on the back. "You were so cool! I would have blown it, for sure."

Andi was about to join in the celebration when she saw Mrs. Harris's face. She was staring hard at the rug on the floor like it was the most interesting thing in the room.

"I'm really sorry, Mrs. Harris," Andi said awkwardly. "Looks like we got your hopes up for nothing."

Mrs. Harris made an effort to smile. "Better to find out now than after the check is cashed," she said, patting Andi's hand.

"We do have that cheese clue, though," said Andi. "And we'll check it out on Thursday for you. Don't give up hope yet, okay?"

Mrs. Harris shook her head. "I won't," she promised, putting her hand on her heart. "I can feel it in here. Raisin will come back to us. I have faith in you!"

"I wish I felt like we deserved that faith," Andi said glumly as they rode away on their bikes. "I feel so stupid, falling for that faker. I didn't even think to ask him anything to prove he had Raisin the first time he called!"

"You can't learn from your mistakes unless you make 'em," Tristan said with a shrug as he jumped his skateboard up onto the curb. "Don't worry about it, Andi. We have Gold TV to look forward to tomorrow. Let's focus on that instead. We need some happy thoughts right now."

Happy thoughts, Andi told herself, feeling sick as she rode ahead of the others. All this effort, and they were no closer to finding Raisin. If only she had some happy thoughts to think!

CHAPTER NINE

The studios at Gold TV weren't quite as grand as Andi had imagined them. She'd had visions of a giant movie lot with famous actors scooting about in golf carts, like the tour of Universal Studios her dad had taken her on last summer. She stood on the curb where Mrs. Peters had dropped them off and stared up at a modest, square building with tinted bronze windows in front of her.

"I kind of thought it would be bigger," she murmured to Natalie.

"It beats the Orchard Park library," Natalie replied, tugging impatiently on Andi's sleeve. "If I'd had to check one more microfiche about snow in July or lightning striking a farmer's cow, I think I'd have gone crazy."

Andi followed Natalie up the steps. Tristan was already inside, talking to a petite red-haired woman carrying a clipboard.

"I'm Pam O'Shea, Mr. Goldman's assistant," she introduced herself. "Mr. Goldman called and asked me to show you around. Is this your first visit to a TV studio? You must be so excited!"

"Definitely," said Tristan. "What commercials are you making today?"

"Let's see," she said, checking her clipboard. "We have Annabel's Ice Cream in Studio One, and something in Studio Four, I'm sure of it. . . ."

Andi glanced at Tristan, who was white-faced and tense with hope.

" . . . KittyKins," finished Ms. O'Shea with a satisfied nod. "It's a new cat food line. Have you heard of it?"

Tristan looked for a moment like he was unable to speak. "Those are the commercials with the cute tabby cat, aren't they?" said Andi, filling in for him.

Ms. O'Shea smiled brightly. "Maybe," she said. "Let's go. There's a lot to see tonight."

She clicked away down the corridor on her high heels. Andi and the others followed, talking in low voices.

"You have to prepare yourself for bad news, Tris,"

Andi warned him in a whisper. "Have you thought about what you'll do if it isn't Lucy?"

Tristan increased his pace. "It *is* Lucy," he said simply. "Hey, do you think Ms. O'Shea will take us straight to Studio Four if I ask her?"

"You can't just ask her!" Natalie cautioned. "This is a big favor she and Mr. Goldman are doing for us. We have to go wherever she takes us, or it'll look bad."

"Yeah," Andi put in. "We might look like undercover agents for a rival pet food company or something."

Ms. O'Shea stopped at a set of brown double doors marked STUDIO 1. There was a red light above the door, and she put her finger to her lips. They waited patiently by the doors until the light turned green.

"The red light means they're recording," Ms. O'Shea explained, pushing open the doors. "And the green light means they're not." She beamed like she'd just revealed a major trade secret. "Let's go in."

Tristan twisted his head back to stare down the corridor. Andi knew he was looking for Studio Four.

The studio was dark except for a spotlit set that looked exactly like a beach, complete with yellow sand, a palm tree, and a couple of lounge chairs. The background showed a smooth, sparkling sea. A woman in a bikini was sitting on one of the chairs, holding an ice-cream cone. The ice cream jutted up from the cone like a triple-tiered sunset — red, orange, yellow. Andi's mouth watered as she wondered what flavors they were. Strawberry, mango, banana maybe?

"This is the new campaign for Annabel's Ice Cream," Ms. O'Shea explained, nodding hello to a couple of technicians in black shirts, who were fiddling with wires and cameras. "It's a revolutionary low-fat dessert!" She sounded genuinely excited. "If you're very quiet, I'm sure the director will let you stay on the set."

With a signal from the director, the studio got quiet and the red light by the door flicked on again. The sound of the surf crashing on a beach filled the studio. The woman in the bikini smiled brightly. "Annabel's Ice Cream," she said in a cheerful voice. "All the fun and none of the fat!"

"Cut!" called the director, consulting a clipboard. "Let's try again. I want more feeling this time, okay?"

" 'All the fun but none of the fat'?" Tristan echoed in disgust. "Ice cream *is* fat. That's the whole point. If you want to get thin, go eat carrots!"

There were five more takes. Amazingly, the woman on the set resisted licking the cone. Andi ran a finger around the collar of her sweatshirt. It was pretty hot under these lights. Why wasn't the ice cream melting?

Natalie had to hold Tristan's arm to stop him from running out of the studio and back into the corridor while they waited in the dark until the director was satisfied. The more Andi heard the Annabel's Ice Cream slogan, the worse it sounded. By the end, she and Natalie had to avoid each other's gaze because they were both in danger of giggling.

"If Mom ever thinks of buying Annabel's Ice Cream, I'm going to die," Tristan muttered furiously as they trooped back into the corridor twenty minutes later.

Ms. O'Shea then took them to the editing suite next to Studio One, where they had to endure the Annabel's Ice Cream slogan another ten times while editors fiddled with computers, sound, and color.

"Um, Ms. O'Shea?" Andi asked. "How come the ice cream didn't melt under the lights?"

Ms. O'Shea chuckled. "It didn't melt because it wasn't ice cream!" she said mysteriously. Then she explained. "We use mashed potato in the commercials, and dye it with food coloring so that it looks like ice cream. That way, we avoid the mess."

Tristan made gagging noises in the back of his throat as they followed Ms. O'Shea dutifully down the corridor. "Gross!" he whispered to the others. "I saw a bowl of the stuff on the side in there. I almost snuck some!"

"You said low-fat ice cream was disgusting!" Natalie exclaimed. "And now you're telling us you wanted to taste some?"

Tristan shrugged. "Food's food. I was getting desperate there."

They peered into the empty Studio Two (very small) and Studio Three (very large) while Ms. O'Shea explained about lighting rigs and digital camerawork. At last, forty minutes into the tour, they turned a corner and went through a set of doors marked Studio 4.

Andi blinked, feeling disoriented. There were four different sets in the studio: a kitchen, a garden, and two identical living rooms, one with a strategically placed lamp beaming what resembled bright sunshine through the window, and the second with drawn drapes, subtle evening lamps, and a log fire blazing in the hearth. The garden was very strange, with real plants and a line of washing fluttering in the wind, created by a whirring fan set discreetly to one side. Andi glimpsed a white picket fence and remembered the commercial they'd already seen. This was definitely the KittyKins set!

There was a sudden burst of activity around the evening living-room set. A blond woman in a silk dressing gown lay down on the couch, and a makeup artist rushed over to pat some powder on her nose.

"*There she is!*" Tristan hissed.

"Yeah!" Natalie said, wide-eyed. "I saw her in this shampoo commercial once. I can never get my hair as smooth as she does."

"Not the actress," Tristan said, tugging Andi's arm. "Over there, look!"

Andi saw a crowd of people gathered together in a corner of the studio, talking in hushed voices. They shifted apart to reveal a tabby cat sitting patiently on a table, having its fur combed and its whiskers straightened. *Was that Lucy?*

As if in a trance, Tristan began to walk toward the cat.

"Don't move, okay?" Ms. O'Shea's smile had a hint of steel to it this time. "They're going for a take."

The light flicked to red. The director, a young man with a blond ponytail and leather pants, called, "Action!"

Holding her breath, Andi watched as someone on the far side of the set rattled what sounded like dry cat food. She blinked. *So much for using KittyKins*, she thought, remembering the bowl of canned cat food in the commercial. The cat's ears pricked up at the sound, and it slinked onto the set, leaped gracefully onto the couch, and curled up in the blond woman's lap. She smiled and stroked the cat, who closed its eyes and be-

gan a low rumbling purr. Then it opened its eyes and looked directly at Tristan. Tristan gave a squeak of excitement. A couple of seconds later, it closed them again.

The cat didn't recognize him, Andi thought with a lurch. It wasn't Lucy. It couldn't be.

The blond woman looked up and smiled at the camera. "KittyKins. Your cat will love you for it," she said in a husky voice.

"Cut!" called the director, sounding impatient. "The lighting's all wrong. Dave, fix it, will you? We'll go again."

"Are you still sure it's Lucy?" Andi whispered unhappily. "I mean, she didn't seem to recognize you. . . . "

"There's this noise I used to make," Tristan said in a low voice, his eyes glued to the tabby as it was carried off the set and put back on the grooming table. "Lucy always came running when she heard it."

He made a clicking, creaking noise deep in his throat. The cat didn't appear to hear him — or, if it did, it ignored him.

"What on earth is that supposed to sound like?" Natalie demanded, her nerves getting the best of her.

"A can of anchovies being opened," said Tristan. Andi and Natalie stared at him as if he was crazy. "Anchovies were always Lucy's favorite food. I'll try it louder."

"Action!" called the director just as Tristan repeated the odd clicking noise. Andi was bracing herself for more disappointment — partly because it didn't sound anything like a can of anchovies — when she caught sight of a flicker of movement on the set. The cat had turned toward them, its ears pricked in neat, dark silver triangles.

"That's not in the script," Andi heard one of the cameramen mutter.

There was a pause and Andi felt as if her heart had stopped beating. Then, padding so lightly that it didn't make a sound in the hushed studio, the cat came bounding over to Tristan.

"Hey, Luce," Tristan murmured as the cat brushed up against his shins, arching its sleek, striped back. "It's been a while, hasn't it?"

For a moment, it was as if the busy shoot had melted away and Tristan and Lucy were on their own in the shadowy room. Andi was struck by how beautiful Lucy's markings were. Tristan's photos hadn't done her neat black-and-gray stripes any justice. The markings on her face looked like makeup — long, black lines that snaked out from the corners of her eyes and up to her ears. Her front was snowy white and, as she rolled over to have her tummy scratched, Andi saw that her tummy was a soft swirling mixture of gold and brown. She looked every inch a superstar.

Natalie seemed close to tears. "Is it really Lucy?" she gulped, squeezing Andi's arm.

Andi nodded, not trusting herself to speak.

The director came storming over. "Who brought these people onto my set?" he demanded, glaring at Ms. O'Shea. "We just wasted a take so some kid could pet the cat?"

Tristan looked up from hugging Lucy, who was butting his chin with her head. "She's my cat," he said. "I can pet her if I want to."

"Your cat?" Ms. O'Shea echoed, looking shocked. "That's impossible!"

The director threw up his hands. "Great!" he muttered. "A crazed cat fan. We have two days to shoot three commercials, and now this." He tried to smile sympathetically at Tristan, but it came out as a grimace. "Kid, this isn't your cat," he said. "It belongs to Tanika. Come over here, Tanika. Sort this mess out for me, will you? We're wasting time and money."

A young camerawoman with dark curly hair pushed her way through. "Uh, hi," she said. "You think Mackerel is your cat?"

"Her name's Lucy, and I don't *think* she's mine," Tristan said, sounding firm. "I *know* she's mine."

The director made a sputtering noise. "Do you have proof?"

"Tristan made a memory book of Lucy," Andi said. "There are photos."

"He'd be happy to show you anytime," Natalie added.

"*Anytime* isn't right now though, is it?" snapped the director. He reached for Lucy but Tristan drew back.

"Where did you get this cat?" he asked the camerawoman.

Tanika shrugged. "She turned up at my apartment building months ago," she said. "She was thin, and I gave her food. She's been with me ever since. When we needed a cat for this commercial, we gave Mackerel a screen test, and here we are. She's a natural in front of the cameras."

"Lucy disappeared several months ago!" Tristan said triumphantly. "See? There's your proof."

"That's coincidence, not proof," said the director. "That cat is staying right here."

"But I *can* prove it!" Tristan looked desperate. "Her markings are different on her left than her right. Her favorite food is anchovies! Listen, there's this noise I make — "

"Look, kid," the director said as kindly as he could, "*proof* means something like a photo or a document, right here and now. I don't see anything, so I'm going to take this cat back and finish my schedule, and there's nothing you can do about it."

"I'm sorry," the curly-haired camerawoman said to Tristan, sounding genuinely apologetic. "We really have to finish these commercials. Mackerel is under contract. Legally, she's ours. Please try and understand." And with that, she lifted Lucy out of Tristan's arms.

CHAPTER TEN

Andi crossed her fingers inside her mittens and rang the doorbell.

"Do I look okay?" Natalie asked nervously, trying to look at her reflection in the frosted glass on the Saunderses' front door.

Andi sighed. "We're here for Tristan's benefit, Nat — not Dean's! Tristan looked awful when we left Gold TV last night. He didn't say a single word, not even good night. I'm really worried about him."

"So am I!" Natalie protested, tucking her hair behind her ears and smoothing her bangs. "I just want to look my best, that's all. I can't cheer Tristan up if I don't look good, can I?"

Dean opened the door, and Natalie blushed to the roots of her hair. "Is Tristan in?" she squeaked.

"He's here in body, but I think his soul is someplace else," Dean said, standing aside to let them in.

"Yes," Andi said sadly, unclipping Buddy's leash. "He left it at Gold TV last night. Where is he?"

Dean nodded his head at the stairs. "Up there, looking at that memory book of Lucy. See if you can get him downstairs, will you? He hasn't eaten anything today."

Tristan's door was firmly closed. Natalie gave a tentative knock.

"Go away," Tristan mumbled.

Natalie glanced at Andi wide-eyed. "It's us," Andi called, pushing open the door. "How are you doing?"

Tristan's eyes looked red. He shrugged. "Okay, I guess," he said.

"How's your assignment?" Natalie tried. "Did you finish it yet? We found some great stuff on the net about a heat wave in November that caused a power failure all over the state, with all the air conditioners running."

"Whatever."

Tristan kept turning the pages of his memory book until Andi gently took it from his hands. "At least you know Lucy's alive," she said. "That's great news, isn't it?"

Tristan snorted. "We should be called the 'Pet Finders

and Keepers Club,' " he said. "What's the point of finding pets if we can't get them back?"

"We can still get Raisin back," Andi reminded him.
"We're going to Oakwood tomorrow, remember?"

Tristan shook his head and took back the memory
book. "I'm not going anywhere," he said. "I've skated up
hills, nearly missed trains, fixed posters till my arms
practically fell off. I even had to fake an interest in low-
fat dessert! This detective stuff is getting old. Just leave
me alone, okay?"

There was a knock at the bedroom door, and Dean
poked his head in. "Hey, little bro," he said. "Phone call
for you."

Tristan slumped down into his beanbag and opened
the little book again. "Tell them I'm not here."

Dean held out the cordless phone. "I think you are,"
he said. "It's the camerawoman from the TV studios."

Tristan dropped the memory book to the floor and
grabbed the receiver. "You can't keep Lucy!" he said
fiercely before the other person had a chance to speak.
"She's mine! You have to give her back!"

Andi strained to hear what Tanika was saying, but
Tristan was holding the phone to his ear too tightly.
Then . . .

"You mean it?" Tristan's face suddenly cleared. "Seriously?"

Andi wanted to scream, *What? What's she saying?* Instead, she reached for Natalie's hand and gripped it hard.

Tristan sank down into a chair. "Now?" he croaked into the phone. "Yes! Sure! Yes. Okay. Bye!" He carefully put the phone down and stared at Andi and Natalie.

"What did she say?" Natalie begged, then covered her ears with her hands like she didn't want to hear Tristan's answer.

"She's bringing Lucy back," Tristan said in a daze. "She's coming here in twenty minutes. Lucy's coming home!"

The next twenty minutes passed in a blur of shouting and frantic phone calls to Mr. and Mrs. Saunders, who were at work. Andi shut Buddy upstairs while Natalie helped Dean hunt down a couple of food bowls in the kitchen. When the doorbell rang, Tristan raced to answer it with a shout of excitement.

Tanika was standing on the doorstep, holding a pet carrier. Smiling, she set it on the floor and opened it. Lucy's tabby-and-white face peeped out and sniffed the air. Andi watched as she daintily stepped out of the basket and headed straight for the kitchen. She knew exactly where she was!

"The anchovy cupboard!" Tristan exclaimed as Lucy jumped onto the counter and pawed delicately at a cupboard handle. "She remembers!"

"What made you change your mind?" Andi asked Tanika, as Tristan grabbed a can of anchovies and tugged at the silver tab opener.

"I believed Tristan as soon as he mentioned Mackerel's — I mean, Lucy's — markings being different on each side," Tanika said. "To be honest, I've been expecting something like this to happen ever since I found her. I knew her owner would want her back someday."

There was a familiar cracking, creaking sound as Tristan peeled away the anchovy lid. Lucy let out a loud meow and reached up with her paw to dab at Tristan's hand.

"Hey!" Natalie exclaimed. "That's the sound!"

"Told you it was convincing," said Tristan triumphantly.

"But what about the contract?" Andi insisted, turning back to Tanika. "You said Lucy was legally yours."

"We were under a lot of pressure to finish that commercial yesterday," Tanika confessed. "But it nagged at me all night. So I went to the office today and checked

the contract. She's legally obliged to complete the commercials, but there was nothing about where she had to
live."

"Why is Lucy a 'he' in the commercials?" Natalie
asked curiously.

Tanika laughed. "Oh, that! We had another cat lined
up for the commercial, but he got a part in a movie. So
we used Lucy, but decided to leave the script as it was."

"Won't you miss her?" Andi asked.

Tanika gave a half smile. "Sure," she said. "She's a
great cat. But she's not mine, is she? If I needed any
more proof that this is where she belongs, I think I just
got it." She nodded at Lucy, who was scarfing down the
anchovies, with Tristan crouched an inch from her face,
stroking her gently between the ears.

Andi flew through her assignment on Wednesday night,
even finding some weather graphics on the Internet to
decorate the pages.

"It looks really cool," she told Natalie when they met
on the station platform on Thursday morning. "I think
Mr. Dixon's going to like it."

"I found a cartoon of a cow being struck by lightning,"
Tristan grinned. "I'm going to scan it in tonight. I hope
Mr. D's not a vegetarian."

"Hey," Natalie exclaimed, noticing Buddy at Andi's feet. "You brought the little guy!"

"I thought his nose might help us find Raisin today," Andi explained, bending down to give Buddy a pat.

"That'd be a first," Tristan teased.

Andi bristled. "Well, Mrs. Harris seemed to think he might be able to," she said. "So it's worth a try."

A tall, dark man approached them. "You must be Stuart's friends," he greeted them. "He told me to look out for you."

Stuart wasn't working that day, so he'd arranged for his coworker Randall to watch out for them, instead.

The train to Oakwood was much busier than it had been on Saturday — Andi guessed it had something to do with the market. The stations flashed by so fast that she was amazed when they pulled into Oakwood after what seemed like two minutes of traveling. She was starting to feel nervous. What if this turned out to be a false lead? Then they really would be back to square one.

They arranged to meet Randall on his next train that passed through, then headed out of the station among a stream of people clutching shopping bags and pushing carts.

The first market booths soon came into view, fighting for space along the sidewalks. Hams, pickles, crates of fresh eggs, jams and preserves, and honey filled the booths, tempting passersby on every side. Buddy craned his neck and pulled at his leash, his nose working overtime with all the new and exciting scents.

Tristan sniffed the air. "Cheese," he said. "Do you smell it?"

Andi sniffed and caught the distinctive, pungent smell. "I think it's coming from over there," she said, pointing. "Come on!"

They rounded the corner to find several rows of specialty dairy booths. Each table was piled high with cheese of every shape and size, some with rinds that were almost brown with age, others covered with crushed herbs, and yet others with only the faintest creamy edges.

"P.U.!" said Natalie, sniffing. "Did you change your socks today, Tristan?"

Tristan made a face at her and then turned to Andi. "Do we have to ask everyone about Raisin?" he said, sounding worried. "There're about a hundred different booths!"

Natalie bit her fingernails anxiously. "I didn't want to say this before, but what if the lady with Raisin didn't work at a cheese booth? Maybe she just bought a little cheese one time and kept the bag?"

It was the worst possible scenario. "We just have to hope that's not the case," said Andi unhappily.

They took in the scene in front of them. Most of the booth workers were men, with only two women in a booth at the far end of the street.

"There's no one who matches that guard's description," Andi said in dismay. "I thought we could at least make a start with any brown-haired women."

They looked around helplessly, catching drifts of conversation on all sides.

" . . . fermented for three months, this one . . . "

" . . . a little bit of pickle on the side . . . "

Andi ran her eyes carefully over each booth, one at a time, looking for clues. Everyone was wearing regulation green, brown, and even red overalls. Where were they going to start?

She glanced back. What had caught her eye? Then she remembered. *Red overalls.* Mr. Harris had been wearing red overalls the last time they saw him. Could Raisin have followed someone wearing red, thinking it was his owner? They already knew he was a dog who liked routine and who'd gone to the station on his own when he thought it was time to meet his owner. It was a shaky idea, but it was a start.

Her eyes came to rest on a blond-haired man with a neatly trimmed beard and tired-looking eyes, whose pale skin stood out against the blazing tomato color of his uniform. He was taking something that a guy in a green company jacket was handing to him. Andi noticed with excitement that they were cans of dog food.

"This way!" she hissed at the others, tugging at Buddy's leash and trying to edge toward the cheese booth. "I think we need to focus on red overalls." Tristan looked at her as if she was crazy, but Andi shook her head before he could object. "Just go with me on this one, okay?"

The men were still talking.

"You think seven cans are enough for the week?" the man in the green jacket asked. "We've got some new stock in, I could let you have a couple more."

"No, seven should be okay," said the blond man in red overalls. He didn't sound very sure. "We may not have him for much longer."

Andi jumped. It sounded like the blond man's dog was only a temporary visitor!

"Look at the bags!" Natalie squeaked, pointing to a neat stack of plastic bags hanging behind the blond man's head. They were each printed with a picture of a round yellow cheese.

"I'm sure we have the right guy," Andi said gleefully. "He runs a cheese booth, and he's looking after a dog. He must be the brown-haired lady's husband or something. Let's go talk to him!"

"Not so fast," Tristan cautioned, holding out one hand. "Remember the faker?"

"I won't forget," Andi replied with feeling. "Do you think this guy might want a reward, too?"

"Or a ransom," Natalie said dramatically. They stared at one another, their hearts sinking. Ever since the false caller, finding pets had gotten a whole lot more complicated.

The blond-haired cheese man solved the problem for them. "Anything you like the look of here, kids?" he asked.

Tristan walked over and looked him boldly in the eye. "Do you have any cream cheese?" he said. "My mom bought some yesterday for cheesecake, and our dog ate it. He got real sick," he added.

"Dogs!" the cheese man exclaimed, taking the bait. "Don't talk to me about dogs. I'm up to my eyes with this big spotted critter my wife found last week."

Andi was careful to keep the excitement out of her

voice. "That's a pretty strange thing to find," she said casually.

"You're telling me!" the man sighed. "My wife's always finding stray animals and bringing them to the farm. This one was frightened by some kid yelling at him on the train the other day. I don't know what we're going to do with it. We've already got cows, goats, and chickens. The cats aren't coming near the house. The kids are going crazy because I don't want them playing with a strange dog. Dalmatians are high-strung, I've heard. We're going to have to put it up for adoption at some point. I just . . . " The man paused and scratched his nose. "He's kind of cute," he said with a half smile. "I guess I can't quite bring myself to do it."

Andi glanced at the others, who both gave a definitive nod. She smiled at the cheese man. "We're the Pet Finders Club," she announced. "And I think we could be just who you need."

The cheese man apologized again and again for not having seen the posters — their farm was out of town and they only came in on Thursdays for the market. Then he called his wife, who drove into town with Raisin in her pickup truck. Andi saw the Dalmatian immediately, hanging his head out of the pickup window with the same goofy expression he'd had in the Harrises' photo. He jumped out of the truck with a huge bound, almost knocking Tristan over.

"Stop with the licking, okay?" Tristan sputtered, trying to stroke Raisin and push him away at the same time. Raisin seemed to know they'd come to take him home. He bent down and sniffed Buddy with interest. Natalie petted him from a distance, careful to keep her fake-fur jacket away from Raisin's scrabbling paws.

"He looks okay," Andi told Mrs. Harris on the cell phone, as Raisin lay panting at her feet. "Just a little grimy from the farm, that's all. So, you'll meet us at the train? Great! We'll see you in about an hour!"

As the train sped home, Andi and the others did their best to clean Raisin up, rubbing hard at his dingy fur until the black spots gleamed against his glossy white coat. Andi kept catching Natalie's eye and grinning. It had been a crazy week of pet finding!

As soon as they stepped off the train at Orchard Park, Mrs. Harris came running onto the platform and kissed Raisin all over. "It'll be such a surprise for my husband when he gets home from work," she said, scratching Raisin's tummy as the big dog squirmed at her feet with delight. "Please, come and join us! And do bring those great dogs again. This evening? Around six?"

"Will there be food?" Tristan checked.

"Plenty!" Mrs. Harris promised.

"Oh, Tristan can't come," Natalie teased. "He has to go home and check that Lucy's eating right, and keeping her paws clean, and not eating too many anchovies. . . . "

"Lucy doesn't need me there all the time!" Tristan objected. "I'm just making up for all those months she wasn't there, that's all."

"Yes, well, if I were Lucy, I might go back to Tanika to escape all the fuss!" Natalie grinned.

"Thanks, Mrs. Harris, we'd love to come," Andi said firmly as Natalie and Tristan started bickering. Buddy barked in agreement.

Tristan turned and gave the others a wicked smile. "Dean's lending me his bike tonight," he said. "Hope you're feeling up to it."

Andi raised her eyebrows. "Are you challenging us to a race?"

Tristan's eyes gleamed. "Remember the Harrises' hill? I've gotten into great shape with all that skateboarding up and down. And a bike is much easier than boarding. So, be afraid. Be *very* afraid."

ABOUT THE AUTHOR

Ben Baglio was born in New York, and grew up in a small town in southern New Jersey. He was the only boy in a family with three sisters.

Ben spent a lot of his childhood reading. English was always his favorite subject, and after graduating from high school, he went on to study English Literature at the University of Pennsylvania. During his coursework, he was able to spend a year in Edinburgh, Scotland.

After graduation, Ben Baglio worked as a children's book editor in New York City. He also wrote his first book, which was about the Olympics in ancient Greece. Five years later, he took a job at a publishing house in England.

Ben Baglio is the author of the *Dolphin Diaries* series, and is perhaps most well known for the *Animal Ark* and *Animal Ark Hauntings* series. These books were originally published in England (under the pseudonym Lucy Daniels), and have since gone on to be published in the United States and translated into 15 languages.

Aside from writing, Ben enjoys scuba diving and swimming, music and movies. He has a beagle named Bob, who is by his side whenever he writes.